'Hey,' he murmured appreciatively, 'you're a nurse?'

'Top marks for observation!' Jenny snapped, making as if to push past him, but he stopped her.

'Don't run away,' he protested. 'I feel responsible for your fall, and you've ripped your stockings—the least you could let me do is buy you a new pair.'

'They're tights!' she retorted, and then wished she hadn't because he smiled a very slow smile indeed.

'What a pity,' he murmured, 'Legs like that are wasted in tights.'

Sharon Wirdnam has been a waitress, a photographer and a cook. She then trained as a nurse and a medical secretary and found that she enjoyed working in a caring environment. She decided that one day she would write about romance against the dramatic backdrop of hospital life.

She was encouraged to write by her doctor husband after the birth of their two children, and much of her medical information comes from him, and from friends.

She lives in Surrey, where her husband is a GP.

Previous Titles

SPECIALIST IN LOVE
A MEDICAL LIAISON
TO BREAK A DOCTOR'S HEART

In fondest memory of Betty Shore

SEIZE THE DAY

BY

SHARON WIRDNAM

MILLS & BOON LIMITED
ETON HOUSE   18–24 PARADISE ROAD
RICHMOND   SURREY   TW9 1SR

First published in Great Britain 1991
by Mills & Boon Limited

© Sharon Wirdnam 1991

Australian copyright 1991
Philippine copyright 1991
This edition 1991

ISBN 0 263 77381 7

Set in 10½ on 12½ pt Linotron Palatino
03-9109-46366
Typeset in Great Britain by Centracet, Cambridge
Made and printed in Great Britain

CHAPTER ONE

'I AM quite sure, Mr Fogg.' There was a pause. '*Quite* sure!' Another pause. 'Well, if I do change my mind—you will be the first to know!' Jenny replaced the telephone receiver noisily.

Men! Why did they treat women like imbeciles? They seemed to think that a woman living on her own couldn't make a simple decision. Like whether or not to take out a new and very expensive insurance policy. Perhaps now Mr Fogg would finally get the message. Farewell, Mr Fogg, she thought as she pulled her uniform dress over her head, and giggled.

She peeped out from behind the curtain. It was an almost perfect morning. Well, as perfect as you could get for mid-January. The sky wasn't quite blue, but it wasn't quite grey either—more the colour of the sea just before the sun came out.

Perfect, and far too nice to be starting back to work on a late duty after two weeks away, she mused as she began to button the dress up.

That was the trouble with holidays, really. You loved them and needed them, and they put you off ever going back to work again! Still, it shouldn't be difficult to get back into the swing of things—the ward was always busy, especially at this time of the year. Broken bones were very common in winter, when the roads became slippery with ice and snow!

She fastened the starched and frilly collar of her dress with the small white stud and stepped back from the mirror to survey the results. A great improvement on the pale-faced young woman of two weeks ago, she thought. Her face was lightly tanned from using the sun bed and it made her green eyes dazzle. Her thick dark hair was as neat as she could make it. It fell to her shoulders in a glossy mass. Really, the sensible thing would be to cut it, but she didn't want to. She was sensible about most things, but not about her hair.

She fastened her belt with the intricate silver buckle which had once belonged to her mother. She had followed her mother's footsteps into nursing and now held the very same post of orthopaedic sister on the ward her mother had run for years. She knew that some people thought it odd that she had never wanted to move to pastures new, to venture further afield, or even overseas, but she had always been perfectly contented with her quiet life and her satisfying job—and what was the point of moving away if you were happy where you were?

She loved the feeling of continuity which came from living in a small, stable community. She felt safe and secure where she was, and security was very important to her.

She glanced at her fob-watch. There was plenty of time to walk down to the village shop before setting off in her car for the hospital. She needed a jar of coffee and some water biscuits, but she wanted to buy some fruit for Mrs Jessop. The old lady with the fractured femur had been on Jenny's ward for so long now that to the sister she felt like a permanent fixture. She couldn't ever imagine her going home and, if she was absolutely honest, she was pretty sure that the frail old lady would far rather stay in the bright, cheerful atmosphere of the ward than go home to a cold empty flat.

There was a lightness in her step as she walked along. Despite her earlier feelings of post-holiday laziness, she was looking forward to seeing all the staff again. She had worked with Dr Marlow and Staff Nurse Collins since she had started at Denbury, and she had known them both all her life. She hadn't told them that she was staying with relatives for her holiday—if people knew that then inevitably there would be phone calls if something couldn't be found, or if something needed smoothing over. The ward staff tended to think that their sister was indispensable and, much as that flattered her, she knew that a complete break had been what she'd needed.

She had gone to Bristol for the fortnight, to the home of her favourite cousin, Joan. Joan belonged to a health club, and they had spent the two weeks swimming, playing squash and lying on sun beds, and then had promptly ruined all the good work by eating pizza and hot curries in the evening!

She would just have to watch the calories for the next few weeks, she told herself sternly—although her navy uniform dress hung as loosely as it had ever done.

She walked round the small village shop, and had collected together and paid for her groceries when an unusually loud roar startled her, and she looked from side to side, thinking that the sound had come from within the shop.

Consequently, she wasn't paying attention as she left, and was just stepping out into the sunshine when she collided with a man who was on his way into the shop, momentarily losing her balance.

A strong arm went out to grab her, and she leapt away from it so that she lost her balance completely and ended up sitting on the pavement, the coffee providentially saved, but the oranges rolling off in all directions down the street.

The man was bending down towards her. 'Here,' he said in a distinctive deep voice, 'let me help you.'

There was only one thing worse than making a fool of yourself—and that was having someone witness it, she thought, and for some reason she resented his confident offer of help, and couldn't miss noticing the twinkle in his eyes as he stood looking down at her.

'I can manage perfectly well on my own,' she snapped, moving a leg gingerly and discovering that she had somehow grazed her ankle.

'Suit yourself,' he murmured. 'But at least I can rescue your fruit.' He began to move away in the direction of the errant oranges, and Jenny picked herself up and began to examine herself for damage.

The gabardine coat was muddy all around the hem—at least that could be quickly brushed off—but where she had grazed her ankle was an enormous hole in her black tights. Now she would have to go home and change them. . .

'All present and correct, I think.'

She was shaken out of her reverie by the man with the gravelly voice, who was handing her the bag of fruit, and she looked into dark brown eyes.

'Thank you,' she said rather tightly as she took the bag from him.

'My pleasure,' he smiled.

There was something vaguely unsettling about him, though why she should think that she didn't know. He was tall and powerfully built, with untidy, dark hair which curled around his ears. She noted that the dark eyes were slightly bloodshot and he looked as though he'd used a blunt razor blade that morning—if at all! If someone had told her that he worked on a building site or at a fairground she wouldn't have been surprised, and yet the dark eyes looked curiously intelligent, and the deep voice sounded educated.

She noted the old tan leather flying jacket and the faded jeans which fitted him so closely that they looked as if they'd been sprayed on. Seedy, she decided. Definitely seedy, and just a little bit dangerous. . .

Her eyes returned to his face and she saw that

he was studying her with amusement, but perfectly at ease, as though he was used to pretty girls standing staring at him.

'And marks out of ten?' he queried.

'I beg your pardon?' What was he talking about?

'How do you rate me—on a scale of one to ten?' he asked lazily.

Rate him! The arrogance of him!

'You wouldn't even make it past zero!' she said tartly, as she realised that he now seemed to be assessing her, and she didn't like the way he was doing it one bit. Round here, where people knew her, she was treated with deference and respect— and respect was just about the last thing on the face of this man. The nut-brown eyes had narrowed and he was looking at her in an openly appreciative way, which infuriated her.

'If you would kindly let me pass. . .?' she said icily, but he had barred her way with an expression of concern on his face. A gust of January wind had pulled at the gabardine coat, and it flapped open to reveal the navy blue of her dress. She saw that she now had his total attention.

'Hey,' he murmured appreciatively, 'you're a nurse?'

'Top marks for observation!' she snapped, making as if to push past him, but he stopped her.

'Don't run away,' he protested. 'I feel responsible for your fall, and you've ripped your stockings—the least you could let me do is buy you a new pair.'

'They're tights!' she retorted, and then wished

she hadn't because he smiled a very slow smile indeed.

'What a pity,' he murmured. 'Legs like that are wasted in tights!'

She was so outraged by his audacity that she was lost for words.

'Can I run you somewhere?' he offered, and he gestured with his head to a monster of a motor bike which stood parked a little way up from the shop, and which she assumed had been responsible for the peace-shattering roar earlier.

Inwardly she counted to three. 'I do not allow myself to be picked up by strangers,' she said clearly. 'And I never go out with yobs.' She lifted her chin. 'And now, if you don't mind—you're in my way.'

To her fury, he had started chuckling at her outburst, and without another word she marched back up the narrow street, knowing that he was standing there watching her, and she childishly wished that they weren't oranges she was carrying but very large, squashy tomatoes and that she could hurl one directly into the centre of his smug, self-satisfied face!

As it was, she had to dash to get to work on time, rushing back to the house to pull on a new pair of black tights and flushing furiously as she remembered his remarks about stockings. Fancy telling him that she was wearing tights! What had got into her? And what was it about him that had made her react so angrily?

She often met men who were interested in her

rather understated beauty—Mr Fogg the insurance salesman, for example!—but she certainly didn't let them get under her skin in the way that the man on the motor bike had done. Perhaps because most men weren't as blatant about it as he.

She put her foot down as she sped along the quiet country lanes to the hospital. A police car in a siding contemplated following her, but when Billy Baxter, the young constable, saw it was that cracking-looking young sister from the cottage hospital, he simply flashed his lights and let her drive on.

Jenny gave a sigh of pleasure as she drove up the driveway of Denbury Hospital. It was set in Arcadian splendour amid trees and manicured lawns. Dedicated groups of helpers kept the flowerbeds far brighter and more lovingly tended than any paid gardener would have done, and already, in the shaded area near the entrance porch, she could see the showy cerise blooms of an early camellia.

She saw few people as she made her way along the corridor towards her ward. Visiting didn't start until three, and all the patients would be lying on their beds after lunch.

All the wards were named after flowers, and Jenny's was Rose—consequently, all the bed-coverings and curtains were in delicate shades of pink, as Daffodil was furnished in yellow, and so on. She loved the individuality of each ward, and was often thankful that she did not work in a busy general hospital, where uniformity was so important.

She hung up her gabardine in the small cloakroom and quickly clipped on her frilly cap with its myriad tiny pleats. The final banishing of a thick strand of hair which had escaped, and she was ready for anything. She pushed her handbag into the locker and pulled the door shut behind her.

The ward was very quiet, she thought as she walked towards her office, with not a nurse in sight. The girls should have finished getting the patients settled for their post-lunchtime rest and be tidying up by now, but then perhaps they'd had an emergency and the routine had been put behind.

As soon as she walked into her office she could sense that something was different. Indefinable, but disquieting. What on earth was it? There were the usual path-lab forms on the desk, physiotherapy requests clipped on to the board next to the X-ray machine. And suddenly she realised what was wrong: the large red book which always sat in the middle of her desk was missing.

Affectionately nicknamed 'the bible', in reality it was just a book used to pass messages on. It had been there longer than she had, and it was invaluable. If Dr Marlow wanted a new type of treatment commenced and she wasn't around to tell, then he'd write it down in the book. He was always popping into the ward at odd moments, and often she missed him. The red book always sat in exactly the same place and she had never once not known it to be there—but perhaps he was buying a newer version which had more capacity!

She glanced at her fob slightly impatiently. Judy Collins, her staff nurse, should have been here by now to update her and give her a report on all the patients. How unlike Judy to be unpunctual. Whatever emergency they had had, it must have been a bad one.

She idly began flicking through the dietician's clipboard when the sound of someone entering the office made her look up, and she met the eyes of a complete stranger—someone who was obviously a nurse, but dressed in an alien uniform of white with a navy belt and a paper cap. Her fair hair curled over the collar of her dress and Jenny tutted inwardly.

The girl flashed her a non-committal smile. 'Hi,' she said, going to sit down at the desk. 'Who are you?'

Jenny was so amazed that she opened her mouth then shut it again, but speech returned, and with it an irritated tone in her voice which she couldn't quite disguise.

'I might ask *you* the same question!'

The girl seemed to have registered what Jenny was wearing, and her eyes came to rest on her name-badge. She looked slightly taken aback, but nowhere near as embarrassed as Jenny would have been in similar circumstances.

'Oh,' she said slowly. 'You must be Sister.'

'I am indeed,' answered Jenny. 'And now perhaps you'd like to introduce yourself?'

'I'm. . .' the girl began, but the phone on the desk started to ring. She made as if to pick it up, but one look from Jenny stopped her in her tracks.

'Rose Ward. Sister Hughes speaking,' she said smoothly.

'Oh, Jenny—you're back! Thank goodness!'

The voice she recognised immediately as that of Sonia Walker, the hospital nursing officer. 'Of course I'm back, Sonia! What's the matter?' She saw the girl in white watching her warily. 'And where's Judy?' she queried.

Sonia's voice continued to sound worried. 'I need to speak to you in my office, Jenny. Can you come down immediately?'

'But I haven't taken the report yet!' Jenny protested.

'This won't take long. Tell the agency staff nurse that she can go to lunch in about ten minutes, when you'll be back—but I must speak to you right away.'

'OK, I'll be right along,' Jenny agreed, and as she replaced the receiver she glanced at the fair-haired nurse. 'Are you an agency staff nurse?' she enquired.

'Yes,' answered the other curtly, 'I am.'

Jenny nodded. That would explain her uniform. 'I have to go and see the nursing officer—I shan't be long. Can you hold the fort until I get back?'

The girl had dead pale skin and her eyes grew fearful. 'Hurry up, then, will you? I'll drop if I don't eat something soon.'

Jenny could believe that—the girl was so thin

that she didn't look as though she'd eaten a proper meal in months, let alone hours. She couldn't help being a little surprised at the forthright response, though—in hospital it simply wasn't done to clock-watch. Or at least it hadn't been the done thing when she had trained—but things were changing all the time, even attitudes in as strict a discipline as nursing.

She smiled as she made her way to the central nursing office, and waited while the secretary buzzed through to Sonia. Moaning about the junior nurses—that made her feel *very* old!

She was shown into Sonia Walker's office, and Sonia rose from behind her desk immediately, as immaculate as always in her smart blue dress, but with an anxious expression in her eyes.

'Jenny!' she exclaimed. 'Do sit down. I'm so sorry to have had you come back from your holiday to such sad news.'

Jenny glanced at her, alarmed now. 'Sad news? What news?'

'You mean you haven't heard?'

'Heard what? I don't know what you're talking about, Sonia.'

Sonia rested both hands on the desk, her eyes compassionate. 'There's no easy way to tell you this—I'm afraid Dr Marlow is dead.'

Jenny's knuckles whitened as she gazed at the nursing officer disbelievingly. 'Dead? Harry, dead? But. . . He can't be. . .' She stared at Sonia. 'He was one of the fittest men around.'

Sonia shook her head. 'I know. It happened so

suddenly. He was driving to work. One minute he was fine—the next, gone. It was a terrible shock. The P-M showed that he had a massive stroke—he wouldn't have suffered.'

Jenny let her head fall into her hands, willing the tears to stop, but unable to do anything to quench them. She had known Harry Marlow for as long as she could remember. He'd worked alongside her mother for years, and then with Jenny herself. He'd eaten his Christmas lunch with them every year, bar the time when he'd visited his sister in Australia. He had bought Jenny the engraved fob-watch, which she still wore, on the day she'd passed her finals.

Sonia moved from behind her desk to place a comforting arm around her shoulder, and handed her a wad of tissues.

Jenny wiped her eyes and blew ner nose. 'I'm sorry, Sonia,' she whispered. 'It's just come as such a shock. When—when. . .?'

'It happened two days after you went away. We didn't know where to reach you.'

Of course, she had left no word. She hadn't even left a phone number.

'So the funeral. . .?'

'Was last week. I'm so sorry, Jenny.'

So there wouldn't even be a funeral for her to attend. No occasion for her to pay her last respects to the man who had been almost like a father to her.

'And Dr Trentham thought it best not to try and

trace you—to bring you back from wherever you were to be confronted with a funeral.'

Jenny had hardly been listening, but she raised her head a little. 'Who?' The tear-filled, green eyes stared at Sonia, who shifted in her seat a little.

'Dr Trentham—he's the new surgical attachment, replacing Dr Marlow. He didn't think it wise to disrupt your holiday, and I agreed with him. He was right, Jenny. You needed the holiday. Everyone knew how hard you'd been working. What was the point of dragging you back?'

Sorrow, guilt and rage combined to form an icy hand which clutched at her chest. 'This—Dr Trentham,' she spat the name out as if it had a bad taste. 'He had no right to make a decision like that, and I'm surprised that you allowed him to, Sonia.'

'I wanted to do the right thing—and what he said seemed eminently reasonable at the time. I know you're upset——'

'How has Judy taken it?' she interrupted in a small voice which seemed to come from a long way away.

Sonia looked as if she was about to wring her hands. 'Judy has left, Jenny. She's gone.'

Jenny looked blank. 'Gone? What do you mean—gone?'

'She's left. She left when Dr Trentham joined. I think she found all the changes too much. She was only a couple of years off retirement, and I think that——'

Uncharacteristically, Jenny interrupted her nursing officer again, but Sonia Walker could see that the normally cool and efficient ward sister was in a state of shock.

'Let me get this right.' She spoke very slowly, as if checking her statement's veracity while she uttered it. 'Not only has this new doctor effectively prevented me from attending Harry's funeral, but he has also made Staff Nurse Collins leave—after twenty years of loyal service?'

Sonia raised her eyebrows a little. 'I wouldn't have put it exactly like that. . . Listen, I can arrange for cover for your ward for today. Why don't you go home and rest? It's all been a terrible shock for you.'

Jenny had stood up, like an automaton, her eyes unseeing. Sonia sprang to her feet.

'Jenny—Jenny, dear! Let me get someone to take you home.'

With a huge effort of will, Jenny shook her head. 'No, honestly. I must get back to the ward; there must be so much to be done. And I want to speak to this—this Trentham man.'

'Jenny—you won't do anything foolish, will you? He acted in your best interests——'

'He doesn't even know me,' Jenny pointed out coldly.

'Yes, I know, but——' her anxious expression returned '—Jenny, I couldn't bear to lose you as well.'

Jenny managed a small glimmer of a smile, and shook her head emphatically. 'Oh, don't worry, Sonia. *I'm* not going anywhere.'

Sonia appeared gratified by this. 'And you're sure you're up to a late duty?'

'I'll be fine,' said Jenny with more conviction than she felt. But she could think of nothing worse than retracing her steps to her small cottage, to sit alone and in silence while her mind tried to grasp the enormity of what had happened—that Harry Marlow was dead, and that Judy Collins had been driven away by his replacement. She felt as if all the carefully arranged order and calm of her life was slipping into utter chaos and disarray. She felt like a holidaymaker who saw glorious sand beckoning, and then stood in fear as she realised that it was quicksand.

She clip-clopped her way back to the ward in her neat, shiny black shoes, her slim legs in the sheer black tights. She held her head high, her neck long and elegant, the frilly cap perched neatly on top of the thick, glossy hair and she was oblivious to the admiring glances cast at her by an elderly woman who was visiting her husband.

Inside, however, she felt far from serene, and as she approached Rose Ward she hesitated very slightly. Should she have Dr Trentham bleeped and confront him now? Or better to wait until her anger had subsided and she was more in control of her feelings? And besides, wasn't unity the most important thing at the moment? She must gather her staff around her now, show all the girls that she was still in charge, that things were going to be all right, and that they could slip back into their trusted and familiar pattern.

She would carry on as normal. She would take a report from the agency staff nurse and then send the morning staff to lunch. She would wait until they returned before giving a full report to the three staff who would be with her this evening, and in the meantime she would go round and see all the patients, check the progress of the ones she knew, and acquaint herself thoroughly with any new ones. And she would give Mrs Jessop her bag of oranges.

She could hear the murmur of voices as she approached her office, and as she drew nearer she could hear that one was most definitely masculine—gravelly and deep—a voice which stirred a vague memory. She stood in the open doorway of her office, watching for a moment. The agency staff nurse was being shown a chart by a man who was obviously a doctor, since he wore a white coat, and Jenny could see the clutter of a bleeper and a stethoscope protruding from one pocket.

All she had time to notice was how wide and powerful his shoulders looked, how tall and just how much bigger he seemed than the sprightly Dr Marlow. Her lip curled very slightly as she observed the dark hair which curled untidily on to the collar of his white coat.

She drew in a deep breath. She wanted her words to him to be biting, and cutting—she could never remember feeling such a raw kind of anger towards someone she didn't even know. They must have heard her, for they both turned round, the pale staff nurse giving her a kind of non-committal smile again.

And it took some moments for it to register why her heart was thudding away like some primitive drum, why anger and scorn had metamorphosed into total shock.

For no wonder that the deep voice had stirred a memory, because this was no stranger. Nut-brown eyes and untidy hair. The legs were no longer encased in tight fading denim—they now wore dark cords, and these, together with the snowy-white coat he wore, had the effect of making him seem almost presentable.

Her shock was so great that she was unable to tell from his face just what his own reaction to seeing her again was.

Stupidly, she recalled his suggestive comment about stockings, and that became the final straw. The gamut of shocks which she'd had in quick succession since she'd come to work that day proved too much.

She was a fit, healthy young woman, but she knew what was about to happen to her. The strange rushing and hissing sound in her ears; the blurring and retreating of the shapes which stood before her. It had happened to her only once before in her life, and she had been fourteen then.

As her eyes stared at Leo Trentham's name-badge, she felt her knees buckle beneath her, and, slipping to the cold floor, she fainted.

CHAPTER TWO

IT SEEMED the whole hospital had become a theatre, the floor of Rose Ward the stage. Coming round was exactly like the fainting attack in reverse. Jenny saw a blurred figure, which cleared, then retreated.

She awoke to find herself lying on the office floor, fine beads of sweat on her brow, the top buttons of her uniform dress undone—and Leo Trentham crouched down next to her, his solicitous expression clearing as he watched her eyelids flutter open.

'Thank God for that!' he exclaimed. 'I've often had a dramatic effect on women, but that's a one-off, I must say!'

'Don't flatter yourself!' she snapped, and tried to sit up, but couldn't manage it, and, feeling as weak as a kitten, flopped down again.

'Stay there!' he commanded, and without further ado he lifted both her feet with one hand, and held them suspended in the air.

'Take your hands off me!' she cried, but he did no such thing, a look of amusement merely crinkling the corners of his eyes.

'Don't be so melodramatic, woman! Your blood-pressure has dropped into your boots; I'm merely trying to restore your equilibrium.'

23

The last person in the world to do that, she thought furiously, closing her eyes briefly as she felt her strength returning. When she opened them again she saw that he was staring at her curiously.

'You're not pregnant, are you?'

She could have sunk her teeth into one of the strong brown hands. 'How dare you?' she demanded icily. 'I'm not married!'

He gave a low chuckle. 'What a refreshingly innocent remark for the nineties,' he commented. 'It may have escaped your notice that a wedding-ring isn't necessary for that particular act of nature to take place these days.'

'It is—round here, anyway,' she muttered. 'Now, are you going to put my feet down—or am I going to have to scream for help?'

'Scream away,' he answered cheerfully. 'When they come running to see what's wrong I shall simply tell them that you're hysterical, and they'll believe me. I am the doctor, after all!'

'You're not my doctor,' she retorted.

'On the contrary,' he fielded smoothly. 'You're a member of staff who has passed out on hospital premises. As I am the resident doctor, you therefore come under my responsibility. Even if you climbed into a wheelchair and got yourself taken down to Casualty, it's still me you'd have to see. So shut up for a minute and try sitting up, but leaning against my arm.'

What choice did she have? She had never felt more helpless or more filled with rage in her entire life. And then, as she started to feel normal again, she remembered just why he was here, and why she had passed out like an idiot. Dr Marlow was dead. She stifled a small sniff with difficulty.

'Hey,' he said in a ridiculously gentle voice, lifting her chin up very carefully. 'Are you OK?'

She stared at him, the green eyes suspiciously bright, thinking that she was at a disadvantage sitting on the floor, her head against his arm, her long legs sprawled in front of her. She was in no position to give the overbearing Dr Leo Trentham a piece of her mind.

'I would be,' she said coldly, 'if you'd help me up and into that chair.'

She hated having to be dependent on his strength as he half picked her up and deposited her into her chair behind the desk. She simply must snap out of this lethargy which had followed her faint. She still had a ward to run, a long shift to get through and this man to deal with.

'I've sent Staff Nurse off for some iced water,' he explained, and just then the pale blonde returned, in her hand a polystyrene cup which he took from her and handed to Jenny.

She shook her head. 'I don't want anything.'

'Drink it,' he ordered, and watched until she had sipped almost half of it.

She put the cup down shakily. 'Thank you, Staff. Would you mind telling the evening staff to carry on as normal, that I'll be out in just a moment? And could you and the rest of the morning staff go to lunch now?'

The other girl nodded. She seemed pleased to leave. 'Yes, Sister.'

Jenny saw the curiously pale eyes glance once in Dr Trentham's direction before she closed the office door behind her.

Leo Trentham remained standing at the window, an expression of amusement lifting the corners of his mouth.

'I seem to have that effect on you, don't I?' he remarked.

'I beg your pardon?'

'It's just that on the only two occasions we've met you've ended up on the ground. It gives quite a new meaning to the saying "he swept her off her feet"—don't you think?'

It seemed that he actually expected her to join in with his laughter. She stared at him coldly, the anger she felt towards him managing mercifully to dispel the tugging at her heart which being back in this office without her late colleague had produced.

'I can assure you that it would take someone as little like you as possible to sweep me off my feet,' she retorted. 'But I'm not interested in bandying around social niceties with you—if you can call your egotistical attempts at conversation that. I just want to get a few things straight.'

He seemed taken aback by her hostile tone. 'Such as?'

She willed her voice not to have a quaver of emotion in it. Somehow she felt that for him to see her vulnerable would be a disadvantage. 'Such as why you directed the nursing officer not to recall me from my holiday in order to attend Dr Marlow's funeral.'

He looked surprised. 'She asked my opinion, and I gave it. You weren't related, were you? And you'd only just gone away.'

'I'd worked closely with him for years!' She spoke in an unnaturally high voice.

He chose to ignore that. 'I'd already spoken to some of your staff. They told me how devoted you were to your work, how you worked unpaid overtime if the ward was short-staffed, which it frequently was. One doesn't meet with that kind of dedication much these days, and I rather liked the sound of you. And I certainly didn't imagine that you'd look the way you do.'

There was a murmur of appreciativeness in his voice and she was furious. 'Just stick to the point,' she hissed at him.

He shrugged. 'You may or may not agree with me, but I've always tended to think that all nurses need their hard-earned holidays. They feel better and then they do their jobs better. Weighing everything up, we thought it better for you to continue with your holiday. I can't see what the problem is, unless you're one of these super-women who feel that the ward simply can't run without their presence. Indispensable is the word, I think.'

'How dare you speak to me like that?'

He remained unperturbed. 'Oh, I dare all right. You asked me a question, and I'm giving you an honest answer. I'm just sorry you don't agree with me. You may be sister of the ward—but I certainly don't come under your professional jurisdiction.'

She bit her lip. 'And Staff Nurse Collins? What did she say? She knows me almost better than anyone. Did she recommend that I continue on my holiday, blithely unaware that the man who was almost—like a father to me——' her voice broke a little at this '—was dead?' she finished in a whisper.

He moved over to her side then, his face soft with sympathy. 'Hey—I certainly didn't mean to cause you this much pain. I'm sorry if you think the wrong decision was made. But you know yourself that attending a funeral doesn't change anything. You still have to grieve. Don't you think that perhaps you might be misdirecting your grief, and it's coming out as anger against me?'

'You can keep your cheap psychoanalysis,' she said bitterly. 'And please answer the question— did Staff Nurse Collins agree with you?'

'Yes,' he answered quietly. 'She did.'

'I don't believe you!'

'Then ask her.'

'Oh, believe me—I shall. And I shall also ask her why she felt she had to leave so suddenly, but that will be academic, since I feel pretty sure I already know the answer to that one.'

He raised his eyebrows. 'Oh?'

'Because she realised that she wouldn't be able to bear working for an arrogant, overbearing doctor like you, Dr Trentham!'

For one moment there was an answering flash in his eyes, and she thought that he was going to respond with an equally angry retort, but he evidently changed his mind, for he shook his head very slightly.

'Why don't you smash a plate or something?' he enquired mildly. 'It might make you feel better.'

'Then I should get out if I were you,' she said between gritted teeth, 'because if I do choose to smash something it's very likely to be over your head!'

'I'm going, I'm going!' he said, in mock alarm. 'Women with green eyes and hot tempers have always terrified me—and, honey, you are one very angry young woman!'

Before she could screech at him 'don't ever call me "honey",' which she was intending to do, he had slipped quietly out of the door, leaving her sitting there, her cheeks flushed with rage, feeling ever so slightly a fool.

What on *earth* had made her over-react like that? Why hadn't she been her normal calm, unflappable self, telling him that his behaviour had been out of order, and would he mind being a little less familiar in future?

In fact, what was it about the man which made her feel such a strong and genuine dislike for him? Apart from the fact that he was overbearing and quite disturbingly masculine. Something about the way he had looked at her when he had made the comment about women with green eyes and hot tempers, as if he would like to. . . She shuddered very slightly.

She had better stop wasting time thinking about him. Roll on Dr Marlow's replacement, please— the sooner they could get rid of this unconventional locum, the better.

She stood up to straighten her hair and her cap, and to do up the button of her dress. Calm down, Jenny, she urged herself. It was time to get on with the job in hand. She had better have a quick walk around the ward and say hello to all the patients before she gave the report.

Rose Ward, like all the other wards in the cottage hospital, was small compared to those in some large district general hospitals. The hospital itself was unusual in that it had survived its original small state—the current trend to centralise small units into large hospitals had passed Denbury Hospital by, partly because of the vociferous support of the local community, and partly because an extremely wealthy ex-patient had bequeathed his massive fortune to them. An added point in Denbury's favour was that the surrounding countryside consisted of notoriously impassable hilly areas, which often became cut off during heavy falls of snow—and the powers that be had decreed that it was better to have a hospital which was accessible to all the farms and small villages around, rather than risk patients being marooned in transit to the nearest large DGH.

People often asked Jenny how she could bear to settle in such a God-forsaken part of the country, being so young and so well-qualified, but she simply couldn't imagine life in a busy town or city. She loved the simple calm of country life—the predictability of seasons merging into the next, not obscured or deafened by the intrusion of inordinate amounts of cars and machines. She liked knowing which hen had laid the eggs she ate! She liked knowing people she had grown up with. And, above all else, she liked continuity and order.

Sometimes she questioned why it was that she never felt the burning desire to marry and settle down, and produce children of her own. There had been overtures, of course, two from young men she'd known all her life, and one from a doctor she had gone out with while she was training. But she had not felt deeply enough about them to want to disrupt the solitary peace of her existence. Maybe it was something to do with the fact that her mother had lived on her own all her life—perhaps she had liked that role-model so much that she was prepared to choose it for herself. And, when you'd spent your whole childhood hearing how awful men were, it tended to influence you a bit.

She was aware that, at twenty-six, she was considered by some of the younger nurses to be 'on the shelf', but it rarely bothered her. Indeed, she'd had to cope with so many red eyes and such morose behaviour when nurses' love-affairs were not going so swimmingly that she often felt glad that that side of life seemed to have passed her by.

She put a new notebook into the pocket of her

dress and walked briskly on to the ward, fixing a smile on her face, not wanting the patients to see her upset. She saw an answering lift in many of their faces. She could imagine that many of them had taken the news of Dr Marlow's death badly, but, as well as that, patients on long-stay wards such as orthopaedics tended to miss Sister when she went away. A simple fact—the ship was without a captain!

'Afternoon, Sister!' called a couple of the men. 'Good to have you back!'

She smiled her response, and went round to each patient in turn, perching on the side of the bed for a brief chat, and writing down in her notebook anything which she should mention to the doctor.

A wave of horror, quickly suppressed, washed over her as she realised that she was going to have to take every single problem to *that man*. As she patted Mr Walters's hand and assured him that his fractured neck of femur was healing splendidly, before moving on to the next bed, she vowed that at no time would she let any of the patients or other staff know how much she disliked him. That would be extremely unprofessional, and might even undermine his authority. A clash of personalities was one thing. . .

Unless, of course, she thought with a grim kind of longing, unless he proved utterly useless as a doctor—then she would be perfectly in her rights to register a formal complaint about him.

When she eventually reached Mrs Jessop's bed

she was surprised to see her sitting up in bed knitting, her hair looking smart and newly set, and a brand new fluffy pink bed-jacket covering her thin shoulders.

'Why, Mrs Jessop!' exclaimed Jenny in surprise. 'You look absolutely wonderful—and you're knitting! I didn't know you could knit!'

'Hello, Sister,' said the old lady fondly. 'Lovely to see you—and you're looking bonny yourself.'

'Tell me what's happened to you. Have you suddenly learned to knit?'

Mrs Jessop looked bashful. 'Aw, no, Sister! Years ago, when we lived in Scotland, I used to turn out matinée jackets for every baby in the village. I'd kind of got lazy over the years, sitting in my chair and watching the box. That nice new doctor's taken me in hand, like.'

Jenny felt her facial muscles freeze. 'Oh?'

Mrs Jessop sighed happily. 'Oh, yes. Brought an occupational therapist round to see me, he did.'

'But we haven't got an occupational therapist!'

'Oh, yes, we have, Sister—now! Dr Trentham saw to that! Kicked up a terrible fuss, he did, according to the nurses. Said—what was it he said? Oh, yes—that it was "counter-productive" not to have one, that people got better more quickly with expert guidance. Said that, even if the hospital told him it couldn't afford one, he knew a girl who would come in an afternoon a week and do it for *nothing*! Going to start in a few weeks' time, she is—but she came round to see us all and then got me all this knitting wool. Lovely girl, she is, ever so athletic—used to play tennis at Wimbledon when she was a lassie! Imagine that, Sister!'

'Imagine!' echoed Jenny faintly, trying to force some enthusiasm into her voice. She put the bag of oranges into the old lady's fruit bowl, and, brushing aside her effusive thanks, made her way back up the ward, trying to quell the unreasonable feeling of irritation which was growing inside her.

It all made sense, she knew that. Hadn't she thought that they should have an OT for years? Hadn't she politely spoken to Dr Marlow time after time, requesting one? But the kindly, and somewhat elderly doctor had not been in the least dynamic. He had gone into committee meetings and put his case so mildly that none of the board of governors—operating under such tight financial strain already—could believe his arguments that an OT was imperative.

So why did it irk her so much that Leo Trentham had achieved in less than two weeks what she had been coveting for years? She should be glad for the ward's sake. And yet she felt as though her position as leader was being usurped. What else had he changed while she had been away?

She called one of the student nurses over to her, a happy hard-worker called Daisy Galloway, who was on secondment from Denbury's sister hospital—the large St Martin's. Jenny liked her very much.

'Hello, Sister,' grinned the girl. 'You look great! Did you have a good time?'

'I certainly did!' Until I became acquainted with our new surgeon, she thought. 'Will you do the two o'clock drug-round with me?'

'Yes, Sister.'

They unlocked the trolley from the wall, then unlocked the first section, then the section within which contained the Schedule 'B' drugs. Jenny flinched a little when she saw how disordered the latter drugs appeared—bottles dumped haphazardly into the small space, not into the neat alphabetical lines which she favoured. She wondered who was responsible, but she suppressed a small click of disapproval, not wanting to seem overly critical of her staff. There might have been a perfectly good reason for such oversight—an emergency taking place during the drug-round, for example—when all the bottles might have had to be put back quickly and locked, so that the staff could run to the aid of a patient.

With experienced fingers she swiftly realigned the bottles, then glanced up at the student nurse.

'Do you know why hospitals are so obsessed with neatness and order, Nurse Galloway?'

Nurse Galloway cleared her throat. 'Er—I think so, Sister.'

'Yes?'

'Er—it's because hospitals are run a bit like the military.'

Jenny laughed. 'And why do you say that?'

Daisy looked less shy. 'My dad used to be in the marines, and he told me.'

Jenny nodded. 'Well, you're right! Like the services, we tend to have lots of rules, but there are reasons for those rules—we don't devise them just because we want to make more work for the students, or to be awkward.'

'Yes, Sister?' asked Daisy interestedly. She loved Sister Hughes—even though she was a ward sister, you felt you could ask her *anything*.

'Well, if I shouted for you to get me something urgently—a drug, for example, and we always kept our drugs in alphabetical order, you'd be able to find it immediately, wouldn't you?'

'Yes, Sister.'

'Alternatively, if a patient was having a cardiac arrest and I wanted the defibrillator, it would be of no use to us if the last person to use it had left it lying at the bottom of their ward instead of returning it to the corridor between Rose and Daffodil, now, would it?'

'No, it certainly wouldn't, Sister!'

'There is "a place for everything, and everything in its place", to quote the old saying, because the most orderly way of doing things is also the most efficient, and we need hospitals to be efficient. Not, of course,' here she paused and smiled at the junior nurse, 'that we must ever forget that we are dealing with people first and foremost, and therefore if a patient was depressed or worried about something then I'd expect you to find the time to sit down and talk to them. I wouldn't bite your head off just because you'd missed a bit of ward-cleaning!'

'No, Sister,' said Daisy Galloway, and she tipped two ampicillin capsules into the top of the bottle and showed them to Jenny.

'And why don't we tip the tablets on to the palm of our hand,' queried Jenny, 'which would be the most natural thing to do?'

'Because the patient's drugs don't want to be covered in the sweat from our hands,' answered Daisy.

'Even though, as a nurse, you should make sure your hands are thoroughly clean at all times?' teased Jenny, and the junior laughed.

Jenny stood and watched while the patient took the tablets before neatly signing the drug chart. They moved along to the next bed, a new admission—a woman of fifty who had come in to have a hip replacement. Her operation was scheduled for the following morning, and she would probably only be written up for routine pre- and post-operative drugs, but Jenny pulled out the drug chart to check.

She bit her lip in annoyance to see that Leo Trentham's large, untidy signature was scrawled all over it, but what was worse was the fact that he had chosen to write up the drugs in the most lurid shade of violet that she had ever seen.

Nurse Galloway noticed her frown and peered at the chart. 'That's certainly unconventional, Sister!' she exclaimed.

'It's an eyesore,' said Jenny curtly before shutting it swiftly. Why couldn't he behave a little more responsibly? That kind of behaviour was more typical of a medical student than a qualified surgeon!

As they moved down the ward, Jenny discovered that Dr Trentham also had a penchant for writing in emerald green and turquoise—anything, in fact, other than the usual black or blue. Unconventional? He was that all right.

After the drug round the morning staff returned, and Jenny was given the report by the agency staff nurse.

The girl's pale eyes glanced at her slyly. 'Are you feeling better now, Sister?'

'I'm fine, thanks, Staff,' said Jenny briskly and smiled, her eyes on the Kardex, showing that she wished to proceed.

'Fancy fainting at the sight of Leo, although I can't say that I blame you—he's bloody gorgeous, isn't he?'

Jenny was not standing for that. 'I did *not* faint at the sight of Dr Trentham; I had received some very bad news, and I would prefer it if you refrained from using first-name terms with the medical staff—it confuses the students.' Her voice was not unkind, but the firmness of it indicated that she meant what she said.

'Yes, *Sister*,' answered the girl sulkily, the emphasis on her title steeped in sarcasm, and Jenny's heart sank. What was happening today? She seemed to be falling out with everyone. She knew a moment's longing for the days before her holiday, for the easy camaraderie with Judy Collins and Dr Marlow. But she stifled her sigh. Those days were gone now, and she was going to have to work with these new people, like it or not. She attempted to inject a note of friendliness into her voice.

'Of course, we can use first names in the office.'

'Of course.' The sarcastic reply was one of thinly veiled insolence, but Jenny decided to let it pass.

'And what is your name, Staff? Doesn't your agency provide you with a name-badge?'

The pale eyes lacked any warmth. 'All they provide me with is a cheque at the end of each week—and that's the way I like it.'

Jenny's heart sank once more. She hoped that this girl was going to fit in. Most agency staff nurses she had worked with were fine, but she had known of one or two who had very odd personalities, girls who were interested only in the higher rates of pay which agencies provided. Girls who had been unable to find a permanent job elsewhere, for one reason or another. Some had been lazy so that she had had to chivvy them into doing work; they had never found work for themselves—and there was always something to do on a ward—but had had to be asked to do it.

Yet what choice did they have but to employ agency nurses? Nurses were in great shortage and the conditions were to blame. The pay was still appalling compared to many other jobs which required a fraction of the skill which nursing demanded. No wonder that nurses were leaving the health service in droves, to take on boring but highly paid office jobs, their professional qualifications wasted. And other dedicated nurses, such as Ella, Mary and Kingsley—fine nurses she had trained with—had been forced to seek work in Australia, where nurses were respected and highly rewarded, as they were in America and most other countries in the world. Only in Britain were they treated like paupers and second-class citizens, unable for the most part to even manage to buy houses on their meagre salaries.

Jenny smiled again at the moody-looking girl on the other side of the desk. Perhaps she *had* been a little abrupt—there was nothing wrong with the girl admiring one of the doctors, after all, though 'bloody gorgeous' was hardly the way she would have chosen to describe him!

'So what is your name?' she asked.

'It's India,' answered the girl reluctantly. 'India Westwood.'

'India! What a pretty name! And so unusual.'

There was a slight hesitation. 'I hate it!'

Jenny gave up. 'Well, at least it's not boring, like Jennifer!' She glanced at the Kardex. 'Now, then. What's been happening to the ward while I've been away?'

Staff Nurse Westwood gave the report competently enough, although her voice lacked any real warmth when talking about the patients. But then she hadn't been working there very long, and perhaps it was difficult to become involved when you were doing agency work since you never knew how long you were going to stay in one particular job. She could, in principle, be moved to another ward tomorrow, though Jenny knew that Sonia Walker would avoid this unless absolutely necessary—she attempted to provide some degree of continuity by sending agency staff to the same ward.

When the report was finished Jenny took the Kardex. 'Thanks very much indeed, Staff. I wonder if you'd like to send the evening staff in to me, and I'll tell them what's going on?' The phone on her desk rang and she picked it up. 'Hello?' She listened for a moment or two. 'Right. I'll do that. Thanks.'

She looked at Staff Nurse Westwood. 'Mrs Curran is ready to be collected from Theatre— she's had a bit of a nasty reaction to the anaes-thetic, so I'd like a trained member of staff to collect her. Could you go—and ask two of the staff to move the beds round so that she's right next to the office? I noticed that it hadn't been done on my way round.'

'I didn't have time to do it,' answered the blonde defensively.

No, but you had time to stand in the office in close cahoots with Leo Trentham, thought Jenny, but she said nothing. 'I was just stating a fact, Staff—it wasn't intended as a criticism. By the way—just before you go could you tell me what's happened to my red ward-book? It seems to have disappeared.'

'Oh, that!' India's voice was triumphant. 'We don't use it any more.'

Jenny had difficulty in keeping her voice calm. 'Oh? Don't we? Says who?'

'Leo—I mean *Dr* Trentham. He says that those books went out with the ark. He hasn't thrown it away, though—he's put it in the top cupboard by the door.'

'That was exceptionally decent of him,' said Jenny in a tight voice. 'You'd better go off to Theatre now, Staff.'

After the door had closed she sat there for a moment, perfectly still, her loud breathing the only sound to be heard in the small office. The red book! The bible of Rose Ward! Stuffed into a dusty old cupboard because some insolent upstart who didn't even know the hospital properly had deemed that it had 'gone out with the ark'. Just who the hell did he think he was?

Jenny decided that she would speak to Dr Trentham and give him a few home truths, but she didn't dare risk having him bleeped just yet; she felt so shaky with anger that she didn't trust herself not to scream down the phone at him.

She took a few deep breaths to steady herself, and then there was a tap on the door.

'Come in,' she called.

It was Nurse Galloway. 'Did you want us in for report, Sister? Are you all right? You look really shaky!'

'I'm fine, thanks.' She was not going to have all the staff thinking that there was something wrong with her. She was not going to appear unprofessional for the first time in her working life.

'Do come in, girls,' she spoke calmly, 'and I'll give report.'

After report she had him bleeped, and after a couple of minutes the phone rang.

'You're bleeping Dr Trentham?' queried a breathless voice.

'Yes, is he there?'

'He's in Theatre at the moment. He's operating. Can I give him a message? Is it urgent?'

Of course, he would be operating—how stupid of her to forget. What was happening to her?

'It's Sister Hughes on Rose Ward. Could you please ask him to ring me when he has a moment? It's not urgent.'

'Yes, Sister.'

But he didn't ring back, nor did he come to the ward, and she was due to go off duty.

She looked at the clock furiously—it was nine-thirty, and operating finished at six or seven at the latest. She glanced through the Theatre list—the last case had been a simple pin and plate which would have taken half an hour at the most, and she knew that he wasn't doing an emergency because she would have been informed. He just hadn't bothered to contact her.

Well, he could learn that his sloppiness would simply not be tolerated at Denbury Hospital. Small it might be—but its standards were as high as anywhere in the country, and someone just ought to point that out to Leo Trentham.

She handed over to the night staff and walked to her car, having to consciously force herself to concentrate on her driving, and not on what she was going to say to him tomorrow.

She drove faster than usual and pulled up outside the small cottage, still seething as she let herself in.

Drawing all the curtains and lighting a lamp in the small sitting-room, she made her way upstairs. She changed into a soft green dressing-gown and went back down to put the kettle on. She wanted a bath, but not before she'd had a cup of coffee and something to eat. She had been so determined to speak to him that she hadn't gone to the canteen for supper in case she missed him. And he hadn't even bothered to ring.

Arrogant pig! she thought as she buttered some bread.

She was just pouring the water on to the coffee when a loud roaring made her jump. It wasn't just that it was so unexpected—though it was in a village where night brought absolute silence apart from the occasional car leaving the small pub. Or that it was so loud—which it was.

No, it was just that she had heard a sound like that just that very morning, and something nagged at her subconscious.

She heard footsteps walking up the gravelled path, and then the loud peal as the doorbell was pulled. She got up slowly.

'Who is it?' she called, but in her heart she already knew.

'It's me,' answered a deep voice. 'Leo. Can I come in?'

CHAPTER THREE

JENNY put the chain on and opened the door a few inches, peering out from the lighted hallway into the dark night, to find the nut-brown eyes and the smiling, detestable face too close for comfort.

'What do you want?' she demanded.

'Well, I'm not hoping to white-slave-trade you to Latin America—that's for sure,' Leo laughed. 'It's cold here on the doorstep; won't you let me in?'

'What do you want?' she repeated angrily.

'To talk to you, of course—I should have thought that was obvious. But I'm perfectly happy to conduct our little chat from here if that's what you want.' He glanced over one broad shoulder and she followed the direction of his gaze to see old Mrs Potterton's net curtains twitching quite openly, and the young Lornie girl with her new boyfriend stop their embrace at the bus-stop to stare at Knowlyards Cottage with frank interest. Damn!

'I suppose you'd better come in,' she muttered ungraciously, his words leaving her in no doubt that it was the best of two evils.

She pulled the chain off its catch and opened the door, and he stepped inside, wearing the leather jacket and the faded jeans of earlier, his helmet beneath one arm. There was something about him which seemed to make the small hall much tinier than usual, she thought, and she eyed him slightly nervously.

'You'd better go in there and wait.' She gestured towards the small sitting-room. 'I'm going to get changed.'

She ran up the stairs two at a time, and locked the door of her bedroom while she changed out of her dressing-gown and into a pair of jeans which were nothing like the ones he wore—hers were new and neatly pressed. She pulled a slim-fitting cream sweater over her head, dislodging half the pins in her hair as she did so, forcing her to remove them altogether and pull a brush through the thick mass of dark hair until it looked in some way presentable, gleaming like burnished mahogany down to the slender shoulders.

He had been standing in the sitting-room with his back to her, looking at the spines of the books in the old bookcase, but he turned when he heard her, his eyes lighting up when he saw her.

'Wow!' he exclaimed. 'You look even prettier with your hair down! I think I preferred the dressing-gown, though.'

She glared. 'You can cut the flattery—it doesn't affect me one iota! Now can you hurry up and say whatever it is you want to say—I'm waiting to eat my supper.'

He shrugged. 'Go ahead. I don't mind. We can talk as we eat.'

'It *wasn't* an invitation, Dr Trentham, and—

while I think of it—why didn't you have the courtesy to return my call when I had you bleeped this afternoon?'

'But that's why I'm here!' he protested. 'You said it wasn't urgent and I've only just finished operating. I went straight to the ward but you'd gone—and the staff didn't know why you'd had me bleeped.'

'Don't give me that about only just finishing operating,' she snapped. 'I'm not stupid! The orthopaedic list should have finished by seven at the latest—and don't try to tell me that there was an emergency, because the ward would have been informed if there were!'

'Honey,' he smiled deprecatingly, and if he noticed her glower at his use of the word he didn't show it, 'I *was* operating—but not on an orthopaedic case. I finished my own list and there was a very interesting general case being admitted as an emergency. Rob Glover, the surgeon, knows that I'm sitting my Part II Fellowship in a couple of months' time—and he asked me if I'd like to assist him. Naturally, I jumped at the chance.'

'Oh.' It almost annoyed her that he did have a legitimate excuse for having not returned her call. It would have made it even easier for her to dislike him more than she already did, but if he had been assisting in an operation as a kind of revision for his exam—well, she couldn't exactly berate him for that.

He was sniffing the air like a hungry dog. 'Is that coffee I can smell?'

'No, it's turps!' she snapped sarcastically, but to her annoyance he didn't seem in the least put out by her unfriendliness.

'Smells delicious,' he murmured.

'Well, you're nothing if not persistent,' she said acidly. 'Do I take it you want a cup?'

'Nothing would give me more pleasure—well,' his lips twitched with a kind of irrepressible humour, 'very little else.'

Her expression froze. 'If you don't want to be kicked out let me make one thing clear; that I find nothing as tedious as sustained innuendo, so you can keep your suggestive remarks to yourself. Is that understood?'

'Yes, ma'am!' He saluted smartly, and looked so funny that she had to turn away swiftly because for one moment she almost laughed, and she wasn't letting a sense of humour show a chink in her defence.

He followed her into the kitchen, commenting on the jug on the window-sill, and how much he liked the small silk-screen print on the wall. She wished he'd keep his opinions to himself.

She poured the strong coffee into two china mugs and pushed the milk and sugar towards him to help himself. She noticed with horror that he had ladled in two heaped teaspoonfuls of sugar—surely that couldn't be good for him?

Had he guessed her thoughts? He turned to look at her. 'Instant energy,' he explained. 'Very useful for the middle of the night—for when I'm operating, of course,' he added hastily, and then smiled.

Well, the sugar certainly hadn't affected those strong white teeth, she thought, the nurse in her eyeing them critically.

She didn't know whether to have it out with him here, or whether to take the coffee into the sitting-room—yet part of her was damned if he was going to wreck her routine. She had been about to have her sandwich, and she was starving.

'You won't mind waiting while I make myself a sandwich, will you?' she asked coolly.

'Not at all.' He took a sip of coffee and watched her.

She felt very slightly unnerved under his scrutiny, and put far more butter on the wholemeal bread than she had intended.

'Tsk, tsk!' he murmured, almost under his breath. 'I can hear those arteries hardening from here!'

'It's only the second meal that I've had today, if you must know,' she replied archly.

'Then you're doing better than me.' It was the first thing he had said which sounded in the least bit grouchy, and she became aware for the first time of the dark shadows beneath the brown eyes, of the lines of strain etched deep in his cheeks. He had drunk half the hot coffee off in a few mouthfuls, and she noticed that he was now staring at her sandwich hungrily.

'Do I take it you haven't eaten?'

'You do.'

She sighed, and pushed the plate towards him.

'Then you'd better have that. Go in to the sitting-room while I make myself another.'

He needed no second bidding, and as she piled cheese, lettuce and tomato on to her own sandwich she wondered just how she had been manoeuvred into a situation where she was providing a makeshift supper for the man who had not only disrupted her ward, but had been responsible for her old friend and colleague Judy's leaving at the worst possible time when she needed her more than she had ever done.

The sandwich completed, she sliced it neatly in two with the sharp knife and then, with a firm gesture, put the plate back on the small work-surface. Her appetite had suddenly disappeared, and, besides, how could she conduct what was bound to be a discordant discussion between them if they were companionably munching at cheese-salad sandwiches? She took a quick sip of her coffee before marching back into the sitting-room.

To her fury he looked quite at home there. He had removed his leather jacket and it lay folded on the floor, the helmet sitting on top of it like a crown. He was wearing a surprisingly clean jumper in a pale shade of blue, and she looked at it suspiciously, half expecting to see streaks of oil from his motor bike running down it.

He finished the last of his sandwich and leaned back in the chair, a satisfied smile on his face.

'That was, without reservation, quite perfect.' He must have suddenly noticed her stony expression, because he sat up again, a bemused look on his face.

'Where's yours?' he asked.

She remained standing in front of him. 'Something, or rather someone, has made me lose my appetite. I had no intention of sharing my supper with you this evening. I wanted to talk to you concerning work and you had no right to come to my home. How did you find out where I lived, anyway?'

He shrugged. 'Easy. I saw you here this lunchtime. I asked in the shop then.' He flashed an easy smile.

She was bewildered. 'But why should you have asked then? You didn't even know that we were going to be working together then.'

There was an unfathomable glint in the dark eyes. 'Don't you believe in love at first sight?' he asked softly.

There was something so disconcerting about him—the things he said and the way he looked at her—that for a moment she felt strangely vulnerable.

'No, I don't,' she snapped. 'And I trust you're not referring to me.'

The brown eyes were unwavering. 'You know I am.'

'Well, then, you're out of luck, I'm afraid. You're the last man on earth I'd ever fall in love with. And besides—you're not my type.'

'Nor you mine,' he answered quietly, in a voice that sounded puzzled. He put his cup on the small table, an action which heralded a sudden business-like approach. 'Now tell me, Sister Hughes: what did you want to talk to me about?'

'I want to know why you had the red book removed. And whether or not you were aware that it has been on the ward for years——'

'Exactly,' he interrupted.

'I beg your pardon?'

'It's obsolete.'

'It has always worked perfectly well,' Jenny hissed.

'I disagree.' He relaxed back into the chair again, almost as if he was enjoying the argument.

'Well, I am telling you. . .' she began in as stentorian a tone as she could ever remember using in her life.

'Well, don't,' he murmured. 'Don't tell me. Let's discuss it. Like adults.'

Except that she seemed half-child where he was concerned. None of her normal calm responses seemed to be at hand. She was over-reacting again, almost shouting at him. She made a vain bid to control her temper.

'The way you discussed changing my ward in my absence with me? Is that what you mean?' she challenged.

'Oh, honey,' he sighed, 'I've never known a woman as touchy as you before. Shall I explain my predicament, and then perhaps you won't see me as the villain of the piece?'

'You can try,' she muttered. 'But I shouldn't hold out much hope.' She didn't want to sit and watch while he explained, to see his face grow animated, or the moody dark eyes cast out their strange messages, and so she crouched down beside the fire, freshly made-up in the grate, and lit a match to it.

'You have to understand that the ward was in a state of flux,' he began. 'Staff Nurse Collins left almost immediately after Harry Marlow died. The agency staff nurse may be there for a year—or just a day. I was the only bit of stability at the time, the linchpin, if you like.'

She looked up then, her eyes round with alarm. 'You mean that you aren't just the locum?'

His smile was wry. 'Sorry to disappoint you— but my contract is for six months minimum. I'm here for the duration, honey.'

He must have seen the look on her face, for the wry smile remained. 'Is that surprise or disappointment I can see?' he asked.

'It's both,' she said frankly. 'If you'll forgive my saying so, you don't match up with my idea of what a doctor should be. But, personal preferences aside, you were explaining just why you made the changes you did.'

He sighed. 'I thought that nurses were supposed to be more aware of communication skills these days?'

'I am,' she said tightly.

'No, you're not. You send messages back and forth in this archaic book. What happens if they don't get read?'

'They always got read.'

'Maybe by you, as Superwoman, they did,' he parried. 'Too often I've seen mistakes made, things not done, because staff were "too busy" to read the book, or because they thought that someone else had dealt with it. When there's a problem on the ward I want to hear it from the person in change, and when I want something done with a particular patient I'm going to *tell* it to the person in charge—not write it down like some small boy who's writing his homework! I'm planning to come to the ward every morning or afternoon. More if you need me.'

'That's very diligent of you, Dr Trentham,' she said, a strange bitterness creeping into her voice. She felt at a disadvantage with him, and she didn't know why.

'I am very diligent,' he said quietly. 'And I don't mean to step on your toes. I'm hoping that we'll be able to work well together as a team.'

'I shouldn't count on it if I were you!' she snapped, and began to fumble for the light-switch on the tall lamp beside him, but he reached out and the strong brown hand brushed lightly against hers as he snapped it on.

'Here,' he murmured. 'Allow me.' A soft warm light flooded into the room.

She snatched her hand away as sharply as if a bee had stung her, and he smiled at her reaction, but when he looked at her his eyes were soft.

'I can see why you're so against change, you know. Everything's been ticking along nicely for years, and everything's just as it was in your mother's day. You think that to make great changes would imply a criticism of how she did things, but you're wrong—we've all got to move with the times. Small hospitals like Denbury are becoming increasingly rare, and you're lucky to have it—but it's going to be hard to hang on to it unless you keep up with the larger DGHs.'

'Spare me the lecture!' she said coldly. 'And I've already told you what you can do with your cheap amateur psychology. And now, if you wouldn't mind leaving, I want to get to bed—and you've got a long drive back to the hospital.'

A gleam came into his eyes. 'Nice of you to be so concerned,' he said carelessly, 'but I've only got a short stroll over the green to get home.'

What he said didn't make sense. 'What are you talking about?'

'Just that I've rented a very pretty cottage which is merely a stone's throw away. Why else do you think I was in the street this morning? Just think—we'll be able to wave to each other every day!'

Her face was a study. 'But you've got a room in the hospital—why bother renting? Most doctors. . .'

He smiled, showing the superb white teeth which contrasted so markedly with the deep tan of his skin. 'When are you going to understand that I'm not "most doctors"?' He picked up the helmet and the flying jacket and got to his feet in one easy, fluid movement.

'I guess I'd better get going. I'll see you at work

in the morning—unless, of course, you're going to invite me to breakfast. . .?'

'Get. . .get—*out*!' she spluttered indignantly, and he gave a deep throaty laugh as he walked out into the hall and pulled the front door open.

'Goodnight, honey,' he whispered, and was gone, and it took a few minutes for her to realise that he was indeed strolling casually over the village green, his coat flung over his shoulder. She took one final peep out of the kitchen window for confirmation at precisely the same moment that he turned round, as if he'd known she'd be watching, and she saw his eyes glint in the silver light which spilled down from the full moon, saw his mouth widen in another careless smile.

She shut the curtains angrily, blinking as she realised the extent of what he had just said. Not just working with him but having him inhabit the same village as well was just too much!

And then she remembered that he had walked home, that he had left his noisy machine sitting outside and—worse still—sitting out there all night long!

She had done nothing, and yet she felt as though she were concealing some guilty secret, and she trembled with rage as she tipped her uneaten sandwich into the bin.

He must know how people in small places talked, she fumed as she extinguished all the lights and climbed the stairs.

She bathed and washed her hair, peeping out of the window again afterwards as if hoping that the whole incident had simply been a bad dream, that she had just dreamt up Leo Trentham.

But no, the machine stood there, gleaming in the moonlight, a defiant and overpoweringly masculine machine, and she shivered as she climbed into bed.

What *would* the neighbours say?

CHAPTER FOUR

JENNY'S alarm went off at six o'clock sharp. Not that she'd needed it this morning—she had been awake since four, tossing and turning, counting sheep and attempting simple relaxation therapy, all to no avail, because sleep had stubbornly refused to come.

She washed, put on her uniform, had coffee and cereal and toast, forced herself to listen to the news on the radio—when all the time her ear was half-cocked, listening for the sound of Leo's motor bike. Why didn't he damn well move it?

She left the house at seven, and it was still there. She had to walk past it to get to her car, and she had to resist a strong urge to kick it—or scratch it with her key!

Driving along the quiet country roads was normally the most therapeutic of experiences—she loved to note when the new flowers began to push their buds through. Today there were snowdrops here, which would soon give way to the pale primroses which always festooned the banks in spring.

But this morning she felt uptight and twitchy. She hated not sleeping well—usually she slept like a log. And she blamed that man.

She changed down into second gear as her car

climbed the steep road. He had no right to change her ward. No right to live in her village. No right to come to her house. No right to leave his bloody great motor bike outside all night. No rights at all! Well, he wouldn't have—not if she could have her way!

His presence even seemed to have permeated her house, as if his very masculinity had somehow seeped into and invaded the pretty and feminine chintziness of her home. She had found herself moving cushions around before coming to work, pushing the chair he had sat in back against the wall, as if trying to physically destroy all evidence that he had been there.

She saw a flashing in her rear-view mirror and she glanced up, her hands tightening instinctively on the steering-wheel as she saw who it was—Leo Trentham, astride the monstrous bike, his distance indicating that he wished to overtake her.

For a brief second she knew a childish urge to hog her side of the road, to refuse to move over so that he couldn't pass her, but the urge was gone almost before she had finished thinking it. She might hate the man—but she certainly wasn't going to put his, or her, or anyone else's lives at risk by playing stupid games on the road.

So she moved over, her nose in the air, and the machine moved level briefly, and she saw him grin before he roared off in a powerful display of riding.

She watched as he disappeared. Stupid idiot! she thought a trifle unfairly as she moved up into third—if he drove at that speed he'd be lucky to see forty!

He must have rented Cavell Cottage, she decided. It had been empty all winter, since old Miss Hobkirk had gone to live with her niece. She had tried to sell it, but the bottom had fallen out of the housing market, and in the end she had put it up for let. No one had been surprised that it had lain empty for so long—it was too small for a family, and single people renting cottages were not exactly milling around at this time of the year!

Jenny wondered what someone like Leo Trentham was doing in such a quiet part of the world—he struck her more as the city type. Still, with a bit of luck he'd soon find it too boring for his tastes around here!

She arrived ten minutes early for the report from the night staff. She knew that the ward would be frantically busy as there were two patients going down to Theatre, as well as all the bed-baths and washes for the bed-bound patients, but what she hadn't expected was Sonia Walker, the nursing officer, to ring to tell her that the agency staff nurse had called in sick.

'Sick?' exclaimed Jenny. 'What's the matter with her? She looked OK to me yesterday.'

'I'm sorry, Jenny,' said Sonia apologetically.

'But that makes me one down,' wailed Jenny. 'And it's Theatre day—can't you send anyone else?'

'I'll see what I can do,' promised Sonia. 'But you know what the situation is like.'

She sure did. Denbury, in common with just about every hospital in the country, had a chronic staff shortage.

'OK, Sonia,' she sighed. 'It isn't your fault. I'll just have to do what I can.' Which meant, of course, that corners would have to be cut, that only the bare necessities could be attended to. Bed-baths would be brief and rushed. Patients who were disabled but partially mobile would not get walked out to the sunny day-room at the end of the ward until very late morning. And any patient who simply wanted to talk to her, to air a grievance or to express a worry, wouldn't be able to. All the little extras which made such a difference to the long-stay patients would have to be forgotten.

Jenny called the staff into her office. As well as young Nurse Galloway there was a first-year student—a rather slow girl on her first ward, who wouldn't be much help, and a third-year student named Nurse Lawson, whom Jenny hardly knew.

She gave them a brief smile. 'Right, girls. We're going to be extremely busy. We're one member of staff down, and we've three going to Theatre. Nurse White,' she turned to the first-year who was fingering her apron nervously. 'I'd like you to do bed-baths on Mr Lloyd, Mr Brennan and Mr Weeks. As quickly as you can, please. And, Nurse Lawson, if you would bed-bath Mrs Thomas and old Mrs Warner; I know you'll be as gentle as you can with her—she's very deaf, and frail.

'Nurse Galloway—you can come with me. We'll give out the bowls, make beds and then check the pre-meds for the op cases. They've all had early baths, and been shaved and fasted from midnight. Any questions?'

'No, Sister,' they choroused.

Jenny nodded. 'Good. Let's get cracking, then— we've a lot of work to do.'

They all sped off in the direction of the sluice, loading up their trolleys with bowls, cloths and towels. Jenny and Daisy Galloway handed out bowls to those who could wash themselves—two of them young men, injured on a motorcycle, who were immobilised through traction.

'Nurse Galloway or I will come back and help you with the bits you can't reach—and to make your beds for you,' she told each of them.

Daisy was delighted to be working with Sister and rushed into the linen-cupboard to load up the trolley for bed-making.

They whizzed up and down, changing sheets only when necessary because linen, as usual, was scarce. Jenny sighed as she surveyed the few sheets and pillowcases on the trolley.

'Are these all we've got?' she asked.

Daisy nodded. 'All we can spare, Sister— especially with the Theatre packs to make up.'

'Sometimes I feel as though we're working in the front line of a battle zone!' Jenny quipped, not wanting the junior nurse to see how disheartened she felt.

They made the beds in that fluid way which nurses had, moving in perfect sychronisation up and down the bed, loosening sheets and folding them into three, before folding them over and pulling them tightly over the mattress.

She didn't see him standing there for a moment, and when she did notice him she stood up too swiftly, catching the edge of her frilly cap on the back-rest of the bed, dislodging a pin, so that a thick lock of the dark shiny hair flopped out of the bun on to her cheek. A tanned hand reached up before she could stop it, and deftly tucked it behind her ear.

'Allow me,' Leo smiled.

Jenny went white with rage. 'Would you mind moving the dirty-linen skip back into the sluice, Nurse Galloway?' she asked in a tight, controlled voice.

'Yes, Sister,' answered Daisy gleefully.

Jenny's green eyes flashed with fire.

'I love it when you're mad,' he said.

'Don't *ever* do that again,' she said in a quietly dangerous voice. 'Not in front of my juniors, and the patients.'

'You mean you wouldn't mind if I did it in private?' he teased.

'You know that's not what I mean!' she retorted. 'Now, what do you want? Can't you see how busy we are?'

'Of course I can. Just thought I'd pop in before I went up to Theatre to see if there were any problems.'

There weren't until you arrived, she thought. 'No problems. All three cases are consented, awaiting pre-meds, and ready to go.'

He nodded. 'I'll come back later, to go round with you.'

'Very well.' She watched him walk up the ward, his white coat swinging, his walk easy. Clearly, the patients found him a lot more accessible than they had done old Dr Marlow, since several of them called out greetings to him. Many doctors liked to keep an enormous distance between themselves and the patients, which the patients often found daunting and intimidating. Not Leo Trentham, though. She just wished that he'd keep a bit more distance from *her*.

He was obviously one of those men who enjoyed a challenge, and just because she hadn't responded to his ghastly flirtatiousness he was going out of his way to annoy and embarrass her. And he was succeeding, wasn't he? She was playing right into his hands.

She braced her shoulders as she went into the clinic room to fetch the syringe, swab and needles. She had enough on her plate to think about this morning without adding Leo Trentham to the list!

She and Daisy Galloway went into the office to the dangerous-drugs cupboard, as it was still old-fashionedly known—although the correct term was now 'controlled drugs'. These were always checked and counted by two nurses, one of whom had to be state registered. As these controlled drugs included diamorphine—more popularly known as heroin—and other heavily addictive substances, they were monitored very carefully indeed. Not only were the amounts registered in a large book, but the injections themselves had to be given in the presence of two nurses. Because of the hugely addictive nature of these drugs, no one person was trusted enough to have sole charge of them, not even Jenny.

They drew up omnopon to make the patient drowsy, and scopolamine, which dried up secretions—essential as a preparation for a general anaesthetic. At the bedside they asked the patient his name, and checked this with the hospital name-badge on his wrist—this was to safeguard that the right patient was receiving the right injection.

The limb which was being operated on had been marked with a blue indelible pen by the surgeon. This was always done, and it was one of the dreaded myths in hospitals that before this marking had become standard practice some patients had had the wrong limbs operated on! Jenny had always doubted whether this was true—but it was a myth she perpetuated to keep the nurses on their toes!

The drug dosage was fairly low, since the patient was a little old lady who had fallen during the early hours and fractured her neck of femur, and she was first on the list.

'Anything you'd like to ask me?' asked Jenny softly.

'Any chance of a cuppa and a bacon butty, Nurse?'

Jenny burst out laughing. 'I promise—when you're back from Theatre and over the anaesthetic

I'll see what I can do!' She plunged the needle expertly and painlessly into the patient's buttock and injected the drugs. 'Right, then, Mrs Zenga— the drug will make you feel nice and sleepy, so just lie there quietly and try to relax. The porter and a nurse will be taking you down to Theatre shortly.'

The morning continued at the same breakneck pace. She had often been on with Judy Collins on Theatre days, and she really missed the capable and experienced nurse who had worked side by side with her since she had joined the staff. At first Jenny had been worried whether the older nurse would mind a younger woman being promoted to sister in charge over her, but Judy hadn't wanted the responsibility of running a ward. Her husband came first. Why *had* she left so hurriedly? Hadn't she known that she would be leaving Jenny in the lurch?

Pushing yet another dark thought about Leo Trentham out of her mind, Jenny decided to ring Judy after work. Perhaps they could meet for a drink, and she would hear the real reason for her departure.

By the time the evening staff arrived on duty, Jenny was keeping her head above water—just! The second patient was back from Theatre and had reacted badly to the anaesthetic—they were having a run of them lately, she thought—and so she had to do his post-operative observations of temperature, pulse and blood-pressure every fifteen minutes. This, as well as give out painkillers and get ready for the third Theatre case.

She quickly handed over to the evening staff and then sent the three students off to lunch.

'I'm just going to grab a quick sandwich and coffee here in my office,' she explained to Jackie Graham, the enrolled nurse who was in charge of the evening shift. 'Could you keep a special eye on the patient in bed two? He's back from Theatre with a very low B-P, and if it persists I'm going to get the doctor to have a look at him.' She smiled. 'You're going to be busy enough with only three on, and Charlie Towers still hasn't had a wash yet! I'd better see to that or the air will be blue!'

This was Charlie's second visit to the ward. A motor-bike fanatic, he had recently sustained a nastily fractured tibia and fibula, and a compound fracture of his tibial plateau. He'd got these when he'd stalled his latest bike and a car had driven into him. As his old and unsafe helmet had been thrown off at the same time, Charlie was lucky not to be in worse shape.

He had been concussed when they had brought him in, which meant that they had had to hold off the operation until he had properly come round, as it was unsafe to give an anaesthetic to an unconscious patient unless in a dire emergency.

He managed a grin when he saw Jenny. 'Wotcha, Sister,' he greeted her. 'Come to tell me I can go for a ride on my bike, have you?'

'If I were you, I'd never get on another motor bike again as long as I lived,' she said grimly, remembering another motor bike, which had spent the night parked outside her house.

She placed the bowl on the table in front of his bed, and watched while he sat himself up with the aid of the monkey pole. She saw him grimace as he did so.

'All right, are you, Charlie?' she asked gently.

'Yeah, I'm fine, Sister.'

'Keep doing all the exercises the physio's shown you, won't you?' she warned. 'If you're stuck in bed all the time you're at risk of some nasty side-effects. So deep breathing is a must, and so is wriggling your toes, and those circular movements with your ankles, too. You know all that, don't you?'

'Yes, Sister,' he said meekly.

'Now lift up your bottom while I put this clean sheet underneath.'

He complied, but out of the corner of her eye she saw his face contort into a brief spasm. After she had smoothed the sheet beneath him she moved to the end of the bed and picked up his drug chart.

'Got any pain, Charlie?' she asked casually.

He opened his eyes hurriedly. 'No—I'm doing just fine, Sister.'

She moved closer. 'Well, I'm not sure I believe you, Charlie. You've broken three bones in your legs very recently—that's a lot of mending your body's got to do, and it won't do it as efficiently if you're using up a lot of energy trying to cope with the pain. *And* you've got physio in about an

hour—you'll do it much better if you're pain-free.'
Her mouth softened into a smile, and for a
moment she looked hardly any older than the
pale-faced teenager who lay on the bed. 'There's
nothing wrong with taking medication, Charlie—
it isn't brave to suffer, truly it isn't.'

'You should trying telling some of the other
nurses that!' He gave a small grin.

'Who?' she asked gently. 'What was said?'

He shrugged. 'You know the kind of thing,
Sister. "Big strong lad like you doesn't need any
tablets."'

'Who said that?' she repeated quietly.

'Can't remember, Sister.'

'Hmm,' said Jenny. 'I'll get you something now.'
She would have to have a general talk with the
staff at report time. She hated the attitude which
existed in some nurses that there was something
wrong with a patient who asked for regular medication. She'd read a lot about the psychology of
pain, and she knew how much the presence of
chronic or acute pain often prevented a full
recovery.

She checked the two painkillers with Nurse
Galloway, and took them to Charlie, who swallowed them gratefully.

Just at that moment there was a rustle of the
curtains and Leo Trentham breezed in, wearing
his Theatre greens underneath his white coat.

'Hello, Sister! Hello, Charlie! How's the leg?'

'Not bad, Doc! How's your Norton?'

Leo chuckled. 'I'll let you have a go on her—
when you've learnt to handle a bike!'

Charlie gave a rueful smile. 'Point taken, Doc.
You look very pleased with yourself today.'

'Oh, I am,' agreed Leo. 'The world, from where
I'm standing, looks very good indeed.' His eyes
lingered fractionally on Jenny, at the curve of her
bust, the tiny waist which swelled into the slender
roundness of her hips. She felt the back of her
neck grow pink, and she stared at him mutinously.

'Can I help you, Dr Trentham? As you can see,
I'm rather busy in here,' she added pointedly.

'I just wondered if you'd come round with me?'
he asked.

'Not until I've finished this, I'm afraid. Unless,
of course, it's really urgent?'

'No. I'll wait.' He smiled. 'I've some drugs to
write up. I'll see you in the office.'

Jenny finished helping Charlie, nodding and
chatting to him automatically, but her mind was
on other things. Leo Trentham was affecting her,
without a doubt. He was everything that she
despised in a man—scruffy, suggestive, overbearing and brimming over with a sickening confi-
dence. And yet. . .and yet he had her blushing
like a schoolgirl when he looked at her that way.

He had not been the first man to look at her like
that, and he probably wouldn't be the last, but her
reaction to it was unique. Hand in hand with the
resentment she felt at his obvious appraisal went a
strange kind of awareness of herself, a tingling kind
of sensation, a growing curiosity. The beginning of

a mystery which frightened her as it overwhelmed her.

She walked back to the office reluctantly. Leo was seated at the desk, busy writing up some drugs, the slightly too-long hair curling untidily on to the collar of his white coat. He looked up as she entered and the nut-brown eyes crinkled at the corners. She found herself wanting to give him an answering smile, an urge she strongly resisted. How strange that she could dislike him so intensely, and yet be disarmed by the friendly grin all at the same time. She noticed the pen he was using.

'Do you have to write on the charts in that revolting colour?' she asked witheringly.

He let out an exaggerated sigh. 'Here we go again! And pray tell me, sweet-tempered one, what valid objections could you possibly have to my brightening up the drug charts—other than the fact that it's me?'

'It's unprofessional,' she said tightly.

'Unprofessional—pah! Don't give me that rubbish! Unprofessional is not caring for patients properly. Unprofessional is compromising care. Unprofessional is not admitting when you don't know something and being afraid to ask—so don't talk to me about unprofessional! What you really mean is, why don't I conform to the petty little rules which exist in hospitals for no better reason than that some mealy-mouthed nursing officer invented them because she wanted to see the world coloured in shades of grey?' For once the firm lips were not smiling.

'To be honest with you, Sister Hughes—I use brightly coloured pens because the colours cheer me up. I find that hospitals can be gloomy enough places without our help. Now what can possibly upset you about that? I'd like to know what makes you so uptight?'

'*You* do!' she spat. 'I resent your interference and your high-handedness. And in future would you mind not leaving your motor bike outside my cottage all night long?'

'Oh, why?' He seemed genuinely taken aback. 'I thought it would wake the whole place up if I moved it so late.'

It seemed a reasonable enough explanation, but she didn't believe a word of it. 'Oh, sure! You didn't stop to think for a moment what that might do for my reputation?'

The meaning of her words at last seemed to dawn on him, but to her anger he didn't appear in the least repentant. Instead, that slow, lazy smile spread over his face, and the brown eyes glinted.

'I see. Well, it seems a pity to get all of the blame without any of the pleasure. What say I come over this evening—and we'll ruin your reputation properly?'

For a split-second she actually considered slapping his face—indeed, she felt her hand make the slightest involuntary movement at her side—then some measure of her normal self took over again, and she reminded herself of what she had decided earlier. She was playing into his hands. Men like Leo Trentham, who liked to tease and ruffle a woman's feathers, would soon stop if there was no reaction.

She gave him a bored, chilly smile. 'Exactly the kind of remark I might have expected from someone so puerile. And now—if you've quite finished your dazzling display of artwork—didn't you say that you wanted me to go round with you?'

To her surprise he stood up immediately, the mocking smile had vanished, and she had his full attention.

'Please.'

She marched briskly on to the ward, letting him follow behind her at his own pace. She had reached the foot of the first bed and turned round to face him, irritated by the behaviour of two of the student nurses, who both made great mooning faces at him as they passed, glassy eyes with faraway expressions in them. Not that he took any notice of them, she was forced to concede grudgingly, but no wonder his ego was so colossal if that was the effect he had on women.

'Right then, Sister,' he said formally, and she had to admit to herself that it sounded a little foolish. She had always been 'Jenny' to Dr Marlow. 'How are my patients?'

The ward was busy. There were two fractured tibia and fibulas, and a young girl who had slipped a disc through lifting awkwardly. Leo stopped in front of her bed and smiled.

'How are you feeling?'

The girl gazed up at him adoringly. More starry eyes, thought Jenny unreasonably.

'Oh, I feel much better than when I came in, Doctor—but I don't know how much more I can stand of lying here like a lemon! What's going to happen with me, and when can I get up?'

'We're going to continue with the flat bed-rest for another couple of weeks—I know it's a bore, but I don't want to operate unless I have to.'

'I just hate having to ask the nurses to do everything for me,' said the young girl diffidently. 'It can't be very nice for them——'

'That's what we're here for, Sally,' interrupted Jenny gently. 'And we don't mind a bit, honestly.'

'And won't it be worth it,' smiled Leo, 'if your obeying all these kind nurses means we can avoid operating on you?'

'Is the operation dangerous, then, Doctor?' There was no mistaking the fear in her voice.

Leo chose his words carefully. 'No operation is without danger,' he said slowly. 'It's an invasive procedure and is usually performed under a general anaesthetic, and there are potential risks connected with both these things. But you can stop looking so worried—if we have to operate the statistics are on your side. You're young, fit and healthy.'

'I was,' she answered glumly, and he laughed.

'You don't smoke, do you?'

'Yeuk, no!' she replied emphatically.

'Good. And you're not overweight. So operatively you're what we surgeons call a "good risk". But, as I said, stay flat on your back and we'll try to avoid the operation.'

'And keep doing the deep breathing and ankle exercises the physio has shown you,' said Jenny.

'Yes, Sister. Thank you very much,' breathed the girl happily.

They moved round the ward and, while Jenny was looking very hard for something to fault him on, she was forced to come to the conclusion that he was a very able doctor. And he had a remarkable gift for communication. She watched as he changed his approach depending on whom he was speaking to. Towards the little old lady with the fractured neck of femur he behaved almost like a long-lost nephew. True, Miss Heslop had been on the ward for ages, and she had a habit of sounding off to the medical staff on how things *should* be done, which often put their backs up. But she didn't seem to put Leo Trentham's back up. An ex-nurse herself, she certainly had some of the right ideas, but they were hopelessly out of date!

He stood by the side of the bed, nodding sagely as she launched into one of her familiar diatribes.

'You must have noticed it yourself, Doctor,' she began in her high, quavering voice. 'Nurses are just not what they used to be!'

Leo looked at Jenny, a glint of amusement in the dark brown eyes, and she immediately picked up a TPR chart and started studying it.

'Indeed, they're not, Miss Heslop,' he murmured.

'They wouldn't have got away with it in *my* day—I can tell you! Slouching around and sitting on patients' beds, instead of getting themselves

out to the sluice and finding themselves a bit of
work for a change, without always having to be
asked!' She drew a deep breath. 'And their uni-
forms. Too tight! Wholly unsuitable! And their
hair! Half of them look as though they've been
dragged through a hedge backwards! Don't you
agree, Doctor?'

'Oh, I do, Miss Heslop,' he chuckled, and Jenny
made the mistake of catching his eye again. He
was studying her with the most deliberate appro-
bation, his glance running down the whole length
of her body, lingering slowly on the fullness of her
breasts, which even the loose uniform could not
completely conceal. His gaze travelled to the tiny
waist, and the slim rounded hips, running down
to the slender length of her legs.

The glance had been so brief that Miss Heslop
had not noticed, indeed no one had—bar Jenny,
and something in the very open masculine
appraisal made her catch her breath and blush
furiously, and she looked down at the chart once
more.

Her views aired, Miss Heslop lay back on the
pillows, mollified.

'Interesting TPR chart, is it?' enquired Leo idly,
glancing at it over Jenny's shoulder, his presence
disturbingly close.

'Very,' she snapped, following the direction of
his gaze, and then saw to her horror that it must
have been upside down the whole time! She
couldn't miss the amused smile which lifted the
corner of his mouth as he walked back down to

the office, and she felt such an idiotic fool that she didn't follow him. She stayed on the ward, checking that all was up to date, until she saw him disappear through the swing-doors.

She continued to work through the afternoon, and had forgotten the time when Jackie Graham, the enrolled nurse who was in charge that evening, came down to the end of the ward to find her.

'Here you are! she exclaimed. 'Haven't you got a home to go to, Jenny? You should have been off ages ago!' She was very fond of Jenny Hughes, though of the opinion that she let her job rule her life. Her expression suddenly changed. 'It was very sad about Dr Marlow.'

Jenny nodded, her eyes bright. She'd hardly thought of him today, it had been so busy. So much had happened in a couple of short days—it was as though he was forgotten already. 'I miss Judy, too,' she said. 'Did she say much to you about why she left so suddenly?'

Jackie shrugged. 'I'm as much in the dark as you are, but I don't know that she hit it off with the new doctor particularly.'

'I can imagine,' said Jenny with feeling.

She was thoughtful as she called goodnight to Jackie and the patients, thoughtful as she unpinned her hair and brushed it.

She and Judy had been friends. If Judy had left in a fit of pique, simply because of a clash with Leo Trentham, then couldn't she, Jenny, try and talk her into returning? Why should one man's arrogance mean that the ward should suffer?

She made up her mind. She would go and see Judy now.

The wind blew back great shiny heaps of hair as she unlocked the door of her car, and she began to smile for no reason other than that, for the first time since she'd returned to work, there seemed to be a light on the horizon.

CHAPTER FIVE

JUDY COLLINS lived five miles to the west of the hospital, in a large village which could almost have been called a town. Jenny had last been there on New Year's Day when Judy and David, her husband, had held a drinks party for friends and neighbours. It had been an enjoyable day, even though Jenny had had to spend much of the time avoiding the accountant son of Judy's next-door neighbour, who had been quite smitten. Eventually she had escaped to the conservatory and had sat there, sipping at a glass of wine and listening to the comforting sound of raindrops drumming against the glass of the roof. It had been here that Judy had found her.

'Cupid's arrow has struck,' she had announced, slightly tiddly.

'Not for me, it hasn't,' Jenny had protested, and they had chinked glasses and giggled like schoolgirls.

Judy and David were in their late fifties, and very close. Their only daughter, Penny, had married an American and now lived in Florida. Jenny liked them a great deal.

The house was small and detached and stood in a quiet back-road, and when Jenny drove up it was in darkness. She clicked her tongue against her teeth. They could always be at the back of the house, but it looked as though they were out—she really should have telephoned first.

It was as she had expected: her knocks produced no answer, and strangely, the house seemed to have a curious air of neglect about it. She was just walking slowly down the path when she heard a voice calling, and Mrs Cavendish, the neighbour—and the mother of the smitten accountant!—came running down her path to lean over the short privet hedge which divided them.

'Hello, my dear!' she said breathlessly. 'What are you doing here?'

'I popped over on the off-chance,' explained Jenny. 'I was hoping to see Judy.'

'Well, you've got a long way to go to do that!' chortled Mrs Cavendish.

Jenny looked puzzled. 'I'm sorry? I'm not quite with you.'

'Perhaps you haven't heard, then, dear? They've gone!'

'Gone where?' asked Jenny blankly.

'On a cruise—to the Caribbean. And you know that Penny's expecting—so they're hoping to stop off to see the new baby!'

Jenny was inveigled into joining Mrs Cavendish for a cup of tea, and she was glad to gulp down the strong brew while she had the whole story explained to her.

'Very unhappy at work, she was,' she said as she offered Jenny a slice of cake. 'No cake, dear?

No wonder you're so thin! Oh, well—it's a shame to waste it. . .!' She took a large bite.

'Unhappy at work?' asked Jenny in surprise. 'I didn't know that.'

'Oh, yes, dear. Unhappy for a long time. And then, what with the poor old doctor dying, God rest his soul, and that new one starting. . .'

'Yes?' prompted Jenny.

'She said that the new one was like a hurricane. Well, David had taken early retirement, Penny was pregnant—and quite sick with it—so they took off. Just like that! Said that it might be a few months, or it might even be for a year, but that they'd write. I expect you'll hear soon enough, dear. Judy was always very fond of you.'

'Yes,' said Jenny, refusing another cup. 'I'd better get going now. Thank you very much for the tea.'

'Oh, won't you stay? Roger, my son, will be home soon, and I know he'd like to——'

'No, I mustn't,' said Jenny hastily, standing up and fixing her hostess with a brilliant smile. 'I've taken up enough of your time already. Thanks again for the tea.'

'Pleasure,' said Mrs Cavendish disappointedly. 'Roger will be so sorry to have missed you.'

Jenny started the car and drove off in a daze. It seemed incredible how so much could change in such a short time. She felt as though the previously firm fabric of her life was disintegrating. She wondered if anything else could happen which would disrupt the ordered calm of her life still further. What had possessed Judy and David to behave so impulsively? Why hadn't Judy said something if she'd been unhappy at work?

And Leo Trentham had been the tip of the iceberg, she thought grimly as she pushed the gear into third and put her foot down. Whatever he had said or done to Judy had been enough to ensure that she left the hospital.

'Bastard,' she said aloud as she reached top gear, and the angry expletive made her feel marginally better.

Almost without thinking, she found herself on the road to Harry Marlow's old house. He had lived in a nearby village of breathtaking splendour—his the perfectly proportioned Queen Anne house which stood overlooking the small pond on which a mother duck frolicked in the late-afternoon sunshine.

Dr Marlow had adored gardening, but as she parked the car she could see that the formal rose garden at the front needed tending—and the grass was badly in need of mowing.

The windows were dusty, and the curtains had been pulled to prevent any light spilling into the majestic rooms inside. And at that moment Jenny felt that every person she had ever cared for had been taken from her suddenly, and without warning.

She wondered who would inherit the house. Dr Marlow's sister, probably. The one he had visited in Australia all those years ago. And she would probably sell it. Sad, really. He had given so much of himself to the area, not just to the hospital through his work, but to the small communities in the outlying villages. And now none of him would remain.

It was surprising that he had never married. He had been a fine-looking man, with a warmth and a gentle sense of humour all of his own.

She felt restless, and just as she was about to drive away she changed her mind, and set off up the main street towards the lane leading to the sloping fields which overlooked the distant sea. She walked briskly, taking great strides as the wind whipped through her thick hair. The air was clean and tangy, and she immediately began to feel better as she continued up towards the crest of the hill.

Here the climb was steeper, and she occasionally had to use her hands to help retain her balance, arriving at last, breathless yet triumphant, to observe the distant glittering grey band of the sea, where tiny, foamy crests of waves were just discernible. She sank to the ground gratefully, the soft grass making the most delicious seat, and she pushed her hair back behind her ears and sat perfectly still, her elbows leaning on her knees, gazing intently at the limitless horizon ahead.

So, it seemed that there was going to be no easy solution to her dilemma, if it could be called a dilemma. She must face facts. Judy would not be coming back like some glorious saviour to gang up with her against Leo Trentham. And Leo Trentham was not simply going to disappear.

So what was going to be the best way to cope with him? Excuse his vagaries and just concentrate on the fact that he appeared to be a first-class doctor, and be grateful for that?

If only he wouldn't make her feel so—so strange about herself. As if he knew more about her than she knew herself, she half thought and then smiled to herself. She was building fantasies! She was getting as bad as the student nurses who fluttered their eyelashes at him whenever he came within a two-mile radius!

She leaned back and lay down on the grass, not caring that it was a little bit damp. She would just have to look on the bright side. She was content with her lot professionally. It might not be everyone's cup of tea, but it suited her. She ran a busy ward and she liked the responsibility, and if she allowed her dislike for one man to drive her away—then where would she go?

She had no intention of selling up and moving away from her roots, and she had no desire to change jobs to become just another staff nurse at the nearest DGH. The only other alternative would be to get a job at one of the small nursing homes which abounded in the area, and she couldn't bear the thought of *that*.

No, she was stuck with Leo Trentham and she must just make the best of it. Ignore the man and he might go away. She shut her eyes.

Her ears were so close to the ground that she could hear the whisper of the wind as it flattened the grass in waves, and in the distance came the sudden call of a bird, alarmed by something.

She sensed that she was no longer alone even before the shadow fell over her, and she made to spring up in instinctive alarm, when the figure crouched down beside her and she saw that it was not some stranger but the muscular form of her tormentor.

Was it just fear that made her heart race so furiously? she wondered, and she sat up, glaring at him indignantly.

'How the hell did you get up here?' she demanded.

He was smiling at her, looking like a man who was very pleased with himself. 'The same way you did,' he told her. 'I walked.'

'That's not what I mean, and you know it,' she spluttered. 'Did you know I'd be up here?'

'But naturally,' he murmured. 'I followed you.'

She was so dumbfounded that her mouth fell open and remained open until she could find words again. 'You followed me?' she asked incredulously. 'But why?'

He was studying her very hard. 'I asked you last night if you believed in love at first sight.'

The way he spoke, the way his deep voice caressed the hackneyed words, somehow managed to convey an emotion which sounded very close to the truth. She shook her head a little before her normal common sense reasserted itself.

'What a lot of tosh,' she retorted scornfully. 'You don't even know me.'

He shrugged, not in the least bit perturbed. 'I don't know yet whether you take cream and sugar, or lemon in your tea, or whether you prefer Puccini to Verdi, it's true. Or what your politics are—and I don't really care. I don't know what you look like first thing in the morning when you first open those amazing green eyes—but I will——'

'That's enough!' she shouted at him, more afraid of her own shaking reaction to his words than of being stranded on the side of a hill with a disturbing stranger—for stranger he was—with such a look of warmth and desire in his eyes that he made her feel naked beneath his appraisal. 'I also told you that I find nothing more tedious than sustained innuendo—so. . .'

'Innuendo?' he queried. 'I can assure you that there wasn't the slightest trace of innuendo in my words. I thought I'd been especially up front with you, wouldn't you say?'

'I suppose you think that's clever?' she asked witheringly.

'No, Jenny,' he grinned wickedly, 'I *know* it's clever! Now tell me. . .' he moved one strong brown hand to pull a wisp of grass away from her hair, and she felt it brush lightly against her cheek as he did so. '. . .when are we going to have dinner together?'

'We're not!' she snapped, scrambling to her feet, brushing away more grass as she did so and standing to glare at him.

'Then how am I going to get to know you better?' he persisted.

The brown eyes were like warm treacle, she thought before remembering to renew her glare. 'You aren't,' she stated firmly, 'going to get to know me any better than our working together allows, and you aren't going to have dinner with me. Is that understood?'

'Perfectly.' He moved a step closer to her, and before she could stop him he had imprisoned her in his arms. She could feel the rough leather of his flying jacket and the warmth of his breath on her cheek. 'Don't fight it, Jenny,' he whispered. 'You want me to kiss you, don't you?'

This was crazy, she thought desperately. She should stop him, push him away, slap him— anything. Anything at all.

'Don't you?' His voice sounded as seductive as a saxophone and she opened her mouth to reply, but she never knew what that reply would have been, for his lips were on hers.

And then she couldn't think at all any more because she had become part of the oldest fairy-story since the beginning of time. Cymbals were crashing, or was it her heart? Night could have become day, or vice versa, because she wouldn't have noticed, and she found herself hugging him as tightly as he hugged her, and kissing him back with a ferocity which startled him as much as it did her.

The grass continued to grow as they kissed. They were fused with the sun and the moon and the sky. They were part of nature and the grand plan she had made for each and every one of them.

'I think I love you, Jenny,' he murmured.

Crazy, crazy, crazy, she thought as she opened her lips once more to taste the achingly sweet onslaught of his.

CHAPTER SIX

JENNY never did have any clear idea of how long
that kiss lasted, or indeed what would have happened next had a large golden retriever, its tail
wagging furiously, not bounded up to them—
making them start, and breaking the spell.

Jenny felt as though she had woken from a deep
sleep, or a coma. She found that her hands had
burrowed underneath Leo's sweater and had been
luxuriously caressing the honed muscular perfec-
tion of his torso, and that he, likewise, had somehow managed to unbutton the top three buttons
of her uniform dress.

Her lips felt swollen and throbbing from the
intensity of that kiss, and she stared at him,
incredulously and guiltily, unable to comprehend
what had just taken place. Her mouth opened to
form words which would not come, and, before
she had time to piece together a sentence that was
perilously close to both accusation and longing, an
elderly couple—obviously the owners of the dog
since it now went running over to them joyfully—
were headed in their direction, but unmistakably
veered a little out of their path when they saw the
young couple and the pose they struck.

Jenny was mortified. She couldn't miss the dis-
approving expression on the woman's face, or the

knowing glance that the man directed at Leo, and she realised with a certain horror that, if something or someone had not brought them to their senses, Leo Trentham might now be in the process of making love to her in broad daylight. She turned her large green eyes to him, and they spoke at exactly the same time.

'You—you—bastard!'

'Jenny. . .'

She turned on him. 'Don't you "Jenny" me! How dare you touch me? Are you like a greedy little boy in a sweet-shop—if you can't have it then you grab it? Or can't you just accept that I'm not interested in you?' She knew that her actions had belied her words and she didn't dare wait for an answer—she was too frightened that he might choose to answer with his lips. Fear and trepidation and desire mingled to give her fleet feet, and she tore down the hill, leaving him staring after her.

She was half afraid that he might pursue her, but he didn't and she had an unbearable urge to turn back to look at him; she fought it. She didn't need to look to know that he stood like a great brooding statue against the skyline.

Before she re-entered the main street she pushed her hair back behind her ears, and managed to discreetly re-button her dress. But she didn't relax when she got into her car and roared away as if there were demons at her back, or even when she was safely in sight of her house, with frequent glances into the rear-view mirror reassuring her that there was no dark-eyed man on a motor bike following her.

When she got indoors she drew every curtain in the place, and sat for what seemed like hours in the darkness, dreading and praying for his knock at the door. But it did not come, and eventually she forced herself into the mechanics of an evening at home. She took a bath. She watched the news. She ironed a shirt and listened to *West Side Story*. She was hungry, but the only thing she had appetite for was a large bar of chocolate, and its richness and sweetness and stickiness was somehow comforting in a childish way. She felt safe again as she carefully peeled off the shiny silver paper and popped the dark brown squares into her mouth.

And amazingly she found that she was tired, and wanted to go to bed, even though she was convinced she would never sleep. But she had been surprised enough by the human body's reactions and resilience time and time again in the course of her career, and she sighed thankfully as oblivion enfolded her in a soft, dreamless blanket.

In the morning, Jenny could hardly believe that it had happened—it had all the qualities of a dream. She had imagined wringing her hands in horror as she remembered just how she had responded to him, but strangely she felt quite calm. Things always looked better in the morning—how many times had she whispered that to patients? And how true it was.

Looking at things rationally—an ability on which she prided herself—she should just regard the whole incident for what it was: simple, straightforward sexual attraction. Nothing more, and nothing less. The most unusual thing about it all was that she should have reached the ripe old age of twenty-six without its ever happening before. She had never known that a kiss could be like that, so that when it ended you felt as though a part of you was missing.

She knew one thing for sure—that it must not happen again. Leo Trentham was not her kind of man, and nothing would alter that. She must not even allow herself to get into the kind of situation where he could ever kiss her again like that. She didn't trust her resistance if he started ladling on the charm again. What was that derogatory term they used about women? Putty in his hands. Exactly.

Her mind was made up. She would treat him with the professional courtesy he merited, and he must be made to believe that her behaviour yesterday was a rare aberration.

And then she completely put him out of her mind, carrying on just as she normally would on a late duty. She strolled down to the village shops, bought her newspaper and vegetables, and prepared a lasagne for a friend who was coming to supper the following evening.

After she had finished cooking she took a quick shower, put on her uniform and made her way to work.

She took the report from India Westwood, who

looked *terrible*, with huge black shadows beneath her eyes, and Jenny wouldn't have been surprised if she'd had no sleep the night before. Still, the report was accurate enough, she thought reasonably as she put the ward keys in her pocket.

She began with the drug-round but, although she worked as swiftly and as efficiently as possible, always finding time to talk to her patients and teach the student nurses, she was aware that she was watching and waiting, and only a fool would have denied whom she was waiting for. She put it down to nervousness, worrying that Leo would walk on to the ward and say something suggestive in front of the rest of the staff. Or, even worse, that he would grab her in his arms in the office, and then what would she do? Kick him in the shins? Scream? She wasn't sure about pushing him firmly away.

In the end, though, it transpired that all her deliberations had been in vain, for Leo breezed in after he'd finished operating. Jenny was in the middle of a drug-round and she half expected him to walk up to the trolley, but he didn't. She waited until she had finished and then went into the office to find him busy writing in a set of notes, still in his lurid violet pen, she noted.

He looked up as she entered, and smiled. 'Hi,' he said, and carried on writing.

She didn't know what she had expected his reaction to her to be, but it certainly hadn't been this casual and rather flippant greeting. Why, she had been rehearsing all kinds of responses, including 'I'd rather not talk about it, if you don't mind,' and, 'Can we just concentrate on work, please?'

And now he was acting as though she weren't in the room!

'Excuse me, Dr Trentham?' she asked frostily.

'Sister?' The brown eyes did their habitual crinkling at the corners.

'Er—did you want to go round?' Now why on earth was she sounding so *wet*?

He rose to his feet immediately. 'I certainly would. You just looked a bit busy when I arrived. So I thought I'd wait until you were free.'

A perfectly reasonable thing to say, so why did it annoy her so much? She nodded briefly and led the way out on to the ward.

His behaviour was faultless. He listened intently to everything she said about each patient, occasionally asking questions, and once even asking her opinion! He was delightful to the patients, and he elicited the usual swooning response from the student nurses, who seemed to find something to do near each bed he approached.

And Jenny was fuming.

There was nothing she could put her finger on— oh, he certainly wasn't as flirtatious as he had been before yesterday's incident on the hill, but neither was he being cold with her. He was being—just normal, as if he too was behaving as if nothing untoward had happened.

'Don't you agree with me, Sister?'

To her horror she realised that he was speaking to her and that she had been miles away. She'd never done *that* before.

'Um, I'm terribly sorry—I'm afraid that my attention wandered. . .'

'Yes, yes, of course,' he said in the same soothing voice that he'd used to speak to old Mrs Williams. 'You must be very tired.'

Her chin came up automatically and the green eyes flashed. Was he implying that she'd been thinking of him all night and hadn't slept well? 'And what's that supposed to mean?' she demanded.

He made as if to take a step back, in jokey alarm. 'Nothing,' he said hastily. 'Just that I know how busy a full ward can be.'

'Oh,' she mumbled, feeling a fool. 'Yes, it is busy.'

The round continued. He made some comments, a few suggestions, altered a drug-treatment chart, even made a small joke, which didn't amuse her in the slightest—so why she forced a smile, she didn't know. And then he breezed off the ward with as cavalier an attitude as he'd had when he'd first arrived.

Jenny felt bereft, bewildered, hurt and angry. There was the evidence of how much he had meant his words of 'I think I love you, Jenny'—he didn't want to know her today! No, she decided— it was far more subtle than that; it was as if he had decided that she was no longer special.

Was he one of those men with dreadful double

standards? Who chased a woman until they saw
that they had their virtual surrender, and then
despised them? Surely not the unconventional Leo
Trentham? Perhaps beneath that rugged motor
bike exterior beat the heart of a suburban mummy's
boy through and through! The thought made
her smile for almost the first time that day, and
Nurse Galloway, seeing it, smiled happily in
response. Thank heavens Sister was back to
normal—she'd been in a foul mood all afternoon
and no one knew why. Daisy began heaping
liberal spoonfuls of sugar into the cocoa jug with
gay abandon as the clock ticked on towards the
end of the duty.

Of course, the trouble with working closely with
someone was that you couldn't actually ignore
them, however great the temptation, and the
relationship between a ward sister and the surgeon
was about as symbiotic as you could get. Jenny
needed him as much as he needed her, and she
was above all else a diligent nurse who wanted the
very best for her patients, and to obtain this she
needed Leo Trentham's co-operation. Not that
there was the slightest danger that he would
withhold that co-operation—he remained pleas-
ant, charming and amicable. It was Jenny who was
mixed up.

She knew that she came over as stiff and uptight
with him, but it was a choice between that or
hostility as a kind of defence barrier between them.
She just couldn't relax when he was around. One

minute he would infuriate her to the point of almost losing her temper when he came out with one of his infamous suggestions on how a change could be made on the ward, and yet she was having increasingly to admit that many of the things he said actually made a great deal of sense. He was about as different from Dr Marlow as you could imagine.

She had had to abandon her red book, since he had adamantly refused to use it, and the face-to-face contact did seem to work as well as, if not better than, written notes, though she would never have admitted it. The only trouble was that he was the person she was face to face with, a face that she was beginning to observe *was*—as India Westwood had once remarked—bloody gorgeous.

But the brown eyes no longer crinkled at her in that flirtatious over-familiar way which had once so irritated her, and this seemed to irritate her even more. She felt so confused. He seemed to laugh and joke with every member of staff now except for her. At times she felt almost an outsider, and that made her resent him even more.

He appeared at her office door one day with a tall short-haired young woman, whose lightly tanned limbs marked her out as a natural sportswoman.

'Sister, I talked to you about our new occupational therapist—but I don't think you've met yet.' He looked at them both questioningly.

Jenny raised her eyebrows. 'I don't think we have,' she answered stiffly, her heart sinking, though for the life of her she couldn't imagine why.

'Lisa Brooke—this is Jenny Hughes, our greatly vaunted ward sister. Jenny—Lisa is our new OT.'

There was an awkward silence. 'I'll leave you two to get to know one another,' said Leo hastily. 'I'll be on the ward if you want me.'

Jenny tried her hardest to sound friendly. 'I'm sorry we haven't had a chance to meet until now.' She smiled. 'I believe that you were appointed while I was away on holiday.'

Lisa laughed. 'If you can call it "appointed". I'm *very* part-time! Leo knew that I was living down in this part of the world, and conned me into doing a half-day a week, and all for a pittance! I wasn't even planning to do any OT—I'm studying for a degree just now—but you know how Leo is! Once he decides to lay on the charm it's like being run over by a steamroller!'

'Really?' asked Jenny politely. 'I'm afraid that I haven't had any experience of it yet—but there's always time. I believe you're using the old OT-room. Is there anything else that you need? You probably heard that we haven't had an OT here for some years.' Not since my mother put forward the idea that cutting down on 'unnecessary' staff was an effective way of cutting costs, she thought. She had been convinced that the nurses were as capable as anyone of rehabilitating long-stay patients to prepare them for their return home, but this wasn't really true. The nurses were just too busy being nurses to find time to act as part-time occupational therapists.

It had been one of the things that Jenny had disagreed with, and when she had taken over she had tentatively tried to find a replacement OT, but the request had been refused time and time again. And now Leo Trentham had managed to achieve where she had failed. She wondered how on earth he had managed to talk the board of governors into *that*.

Leo had come into her office a couple of days later in his usual bouncy way. It had been a bad day at the end of a rotten week. Consequently, she was not in a particularly receptive mood.

'I'm hoping to get old Mrs Jessop into part III accommodation,' he announced, and Jenny looked at him, aghast.

'Don't be ridiculous!' she protested. 'She wouldn't last for a day on her own.'

'She won't be on her own, will she?' he reminded her. 'She'll be in a warden-controlled flat—there'll be someone there to keep their eye on her.'

'In theory, perhaps, but I just can't see it working for Mrs Jessop. She's not well enough.'

'I disagree. Her femur has healed nicely, and her chest infection has cleared up. Lisa says her progress has been splendid.'

For some reason, this reference to Lisa caused her to clench her fist in her uniform pocket. 'She's too frail,' she stated.

'She's institutionalised,' he said quietly.

'She's *what*?' Jenny's voice was also quiet, but there was no mistaking the anger in it.

'I think she's become hospital-dependent, Jenny, and I think if we don't try and re-establish her independence then she'll never leave this place.'

'Oh, it's very easy for you, isn't it?' retorted Jenny angrily. 'You're just the doctor! You say the leg has healed—OK, fine! Let's just move her out straight away, let's not give a thought to what it might do to her. She's been here for ages!'

'Exactly,' he said quietly, the dark brown eyes unwavering.

'And what's that supposed to mean?'

'You really want to know? OK! I think you mother your patients too much, I think that they depend on you too much, and I think it's wrong.'

'Oh, do you?'

He gave her a gentle smile. 'Yes, I do. I've seen it happen a lot. It's the sign of a good nurse—but you're not indispensable, you know.'

She was perilously close to tears now, 'Meaning, I suppose, that you'd like me to resign—so that you can move yet another of your girlfriends in!'

He was looking at her with open astonishment. 'What are you talking about? Oh. . .' the brown eyes crinkled in that irritatingly attractive way '. . .you don't mean Lisa, do you? Because she's not my girlfriend—you've no need to worry about that!'

'I am not worried!' she almost shouted. 'What you do and who you do it with is your business, and your business alone! Now would you mind leaving me in peace? I've still some paperwork to catch up on.'

'Working late yet again?' he chided, but she ignored him.

'So you're agreed—about Mrs Jessop?' he persisted, and she looked up to find him leaning over her desk in that threateningly masculine way of his.

'She won't agree to it,' she stated flatly.

'She already has.'

'You mean. . .' her voice rose again '. . .that you've already asked her?'

He gave a deep sigh. 'I've tested the water, yes.'

She glared at him angrily. 'So you've taken to doing my job for me now, have you? Why don't you come on the ward at seven in uniform and you can help me with the bed-baths?'

'Oh, for God's sake, woman!' he exploded. 'I asked her about the idea in principle first because I knew that you'd try and put up at least four reasons why we couldn't do it, the same way you've done with everything else I've suggested since I arrived——'

'And you've done nothing but criticise me since you arrived!'

'Lord!' He smacked his forehead with the palm of his hand. 'All I've done is suggest some changes, which you'd admit were good ideas if you weren't so damned stubborn! Or is the status quo so sacrosanct on this ward just because your mother—or Florence Nightingale as you so obviously considered her—set it down?'

She was shaking now. 'How dare you?'

'I'm speaking straight to you, that's all. I just don't know how to please you, woman!'

It was the way he called her 'woman'. Something snapped. 'You can try by only speaking to me when absolutely necessary, and you can certainly keep your wandering hands off me in future!' Now why had she brought that up? She saw his face blanch beneath the tan, saw him clench his teeth in rage, and when he spoke there was a look of naked anger on his face which startled her.

'Oh, I shouldn't worry on that score,' he said scornfully. 'I've never yet sunk to the depths where I've had to beg for someone's favours. Pity, though—there was definitely something there. I'm afraid you've missed the boat, honey!' He smiled, but for once it didn't cause his eyes to crinkle, and before she could even think of a biting retort he had sauntered out of her office.

CHAPTER SEVEN

WHY was human nature so fickle and inconstant? Jenny wondered. Why was it that, as soon as Leo Trentham had professed no interest in her, she began to think of him constantly? She wavered between reassuring herself that she had been right to speak to him so sharply, to wondering why she had rejected him so finally, especially when there was, without a doubt, as he had said, something there.

But you couldn't let sexual attraction rule your life, could you? Taking it to its logical conclusion, she might have gone out with him a few times, probably have gone to bed with him, and then what? The basic differences between them would have reared their heads sooner or later, and he would have been off to his next job, with her waving a hankie at the gate of her cottage.

And wasn't she assuming a lot? They might not necessarily have gone to bed. But the shiver and the gap which appeared in her self-analysis told her that you might be able to fool other people, but you couldn't fool yourself. Look how she'd been with him that day, after just one kiss.

She brushed her hair furiously. Dwelling on what had happened wasn't going to change anything. He wasn't going to be there forever, was he? What had her mother always told her? That men were nothing but trouble—and she should know!

But then something happened to make her revise her opinion of Leo Trentham as a trouble-maker. She had a letter from Judy, post-marked St Lucia. It was a long letter, beginning with an apology for having left in such a hurry.

David and I were thinking of a change for a long time, particularly once we knew that early retirement for him was an option. The chance came to go, and we took it! It all happened so quickly, and Penny needs us; the scan says that the baby looks fine!

But also, Jenny, I had been discontented for some time—I felt as though I had been doing the same thing for all my life, which I suppose I had! Dr Marlow's death came as such a shock, but it seemed a natural time for me to go, particularly as I could see that there were likely to be all kinds of changes with the arrival of the new doctor. I can't imagine how you'll get on with him—he seems very dynamic!—but I know you'll give him a chance.

Harry's death was very sudden, and very sad—Sonia Walker wanted to trace you, but Dr Trentham was against it, and I agreed with him. You needed the rest badly—you should get away more often.

You only have one life, Jenny, and you must live it as *you* want—not as your mother or anyone else wanted. I always felt that perhaps we weren't as innovative on the ward as we might have been, more out of habit than anything else. Your mother and Harry were a great team, but in a way it might be easier for you now, with someone new to work with.

If only she knew, thought Jenny. The rest of the letter was news of their travels, but she scarcely registered the words; her thoughts were all taken up with the opening part of the letter.

It had been couched differently, but the words could have been Leo's own. Judy had been gentle, but there was no mistaking the admonishment— reluctant to change, lack of innovation. . . Had she really been so bound by her mother's influence, never daring to try anything new?

And Judy had even agreed that she had backed Leo in not wanting to recall her from her holiday. Whatever else Leo had done, he had certainly not driven Judy away. Her face burned as she remembered accusing him—and he had not troubled to deny it. Why?

The day she received the letter she could hardly bear to look at him—she felt so ashamed, and she thought that he glanced at her oddly a couple of times. She wanted to tell him that she'd misjudged him, but she didn't know how to approach it, and the longer she left it, the harder it became. She just couldn't face him.

But India Westwood certainly had no similar hang-ups about facing him, and whenever Leo was on the ward India was never far from his side. Jenny watched as she cornered him in the office one day, batting the lashes of those pale eyes as she finished telling him about the laminectomy case she had spent the morning caring for, and he nodded as he listened intently. At the end of the discourse she twinkled up at him.

'You're off this weekend, aren't you, Leo? What a coincidence—so am I!' She rushed on. 'I've got some tickets for a rock concert in Bath. D'you fancy coming?'

Leo's expression didn't change, and then he gave India one of his lazy smiles. 'Have to refuse, India—but thanks, anyway.' It was so smooth it couldn't possibly have given offence.

'Oh!' India looked rather taken aback and very, very disappointed, and perhaps he sensed it, for he moved out on to the ward before either of the two girls had really noticed that he had gone.

To Jenny's surprise and—astonishingly enough—relief, he appeared to have forgotten his angry outburst of the other day, and he carried on as normal with her, whatever normal might be. She had to admit that he seemed to be an unusually uncomplicated kind of person, totally without guile or front. She wondered why more people weren't like him, but, there again, it might be difficult if everyone were so honest—how on earth would politicians manage?

Then she started thinking—what if he *had* meant it when he'd told her that he thought he was in love with her? She sighed. Even if he had, it was too late now. She'd blown it.

She began to realise that maybe she *had* been unnecessarily hostile to him when he had first arrived. It was just that she hadn't known how to respond to someone like him. She began to make a real effort to be nice to him, which she actually found very easy. If he noticed he said nothing, though she could have sworn that she saw an eyebrow raised the first time it happened. After a week or so of this unacknowledged laying down of arms she actually began to look forward to coming in to work.

One morning he came in to do his round before operating, and she was struck by how utterly exhausted he looked. He had great shadows under his eyes, and lines of weariness were drawn deep around the normally smiling mouth. Burning the candle at both ends, no doubt, she thought automatically, but her face was soft with concern as she observed him.

She disappeared to the kitchen, her neat rubber-soled shoes making no sound on the shiny floor, and seconds later she had put a large mug of strong tea before him. He looked up at her and blinked.

'What's this?'

'The milk of human kindness!' she quipped without thinking, and his eyes widened.

'She joked! She definitely did, and I definitely heard her! Jenny Hughes has been caught trying to boost the morale of her flagging registrar,' he teased.

'Shut up,' she replied amiably. 'And don't burn the candle at both ends next time!'

He sipped the tea. 'It was worth it. Very exciting assignation. . .'

'I don't think——' said Jenny primly, hoping he wouldn't notice her fixed smile.

'. . .with my textbook,' he finished, smiling.

'Your textbook?'

'I'm taking the second part of my fellowship in three weeks' time—didn't you realise?'

'No,' she answered, a smile so wide that it was dazzling. 'No, I didn't.' She didn't know why, as she went off to do the drug-round, her feet felt as though there were a layer of air between them and the floor.

Whether or not it was a direct result of Judy's letter, she didn't know—but she had decided that she, too, was in a rut. She started a night-class in French, and once a week she went to an aerobics class. She had great fun going out to choose all the new clothes for it.

The woman in the sports-shop persuaded her to buy a very clingy leotard.

'Isn't it cut a little high on the leg?' asked Jenny doubtfully.

'Oh, goodness me, *no*, dear!' answered the woman, smiling. 'You've got such a lovely figure—you ought to show it off! You should see some of the ones who come in here!'

So she bought the lot, and then one night she

saw him. She was just getting out of her car and Leo had obviously been having an early-evening stroll. Her mac flew open and she thought she saw him start a little as it revealed the clinging emerald green leotard with the matching tights and the purple leg-warmers which lay in folds around her slim ankles.

He stopped and shut the car door for her.

'Thanks,' she said, more breathless than after an entire hour's work-out.

'Pleasure,' he murmured. 'You look hot.'

'I've just been working out,' she explained, although it struck her that no explanation was necessary.

'Have you, now?' he murmured politely, and then he nodded in the direction of the pub. 'I was just going for a drink—pity you're not dressed for it, or you could have joined me.'

'I could. . .' she started. She had been about to say that she could always go and change, and then she remembered India Westwood's invitation to him, *and* how it had been turned down!

'Mm?' he queried, raising dark eyebrows.

'I could do with an early night, actually,' she finished lamely, and he nodded.

'I expect you could. Well, I'll leave you to your beauty sleep. Goodnight, Jenny.'

'Goodnight, Leo.'

One day at work, she had him bleeped.

'Yes, Jenny?' he answered.

'Are you still operating?' she asked.

'My assistant is just closing up for me. Why? What's the problem?'

'I'd just like you to have a look at one of the patients—I'm a bit worried.'

'I'm on my way,' he said, and put the phone down.

He was less than five minutes.

'You were quick,' she said gratefully.

'You don't sound that urgent very often,' he replied. 'Who are you worried about?'

'It's Joe Lyons—you did his tib and fib thirty-six hours ago.'

'Yes?'

'I'm worried that he has compartmental syndrome.'

'But he was fine when I saw him earlier.'

'I know,' she said 'but he's been complaining of a loose feeling in his foot all morning, and——'

'Is he anxious?' he interrupted.

'Not unduly. Do you want to do a neurological assessment?'

He nodded. 'Please. If you're right, and the neuro test is OK, we'll have to get him straight back to Theatre. Or. . .' The eyes which met hers were serious.

'Or he loses the limb,' she said quietly. Joe Lyons was twenty-one years old.

He nodded again. 'Have you time to help me?'

'Of course I have. I'd like to bring one of the junior nurses, as well. Doplar's syndrome is rare enough for me to have only ever seen it once before.'

She called Nurse Galloway over to her as she headed towards the clinic-room. As she found the instruments for Leo, part of her couldn't help feeling amazed that he had taken her tentative diagnosis so seriously. While she washed her hands she began to explain the condition to Daisy Galloway.

'Compartmental syndrome is a rare condition which can occur after surgical intervention following fracture. There are four blood-compartments in the leg, and the blood supply to these compartments can be cut off through pressure caused by swelling. The patient complains of a loose, uncomfortable feeling in the foot. Obviously, we have to assess whether or not this is simply post-operative anxiety or not. Dr Trentham is going to assess the patient neurologically first of all, and then he's going to do something called a Doplar test. If this proves that he has compartmental syndrome we'll have to rush him back to Theatre as quickly as possible, and Dr Trentham will make lots of tiny lacerations, like stab wounds, all over the leg, in order to release the pressure.'

'And is it serious, Sister?' asked Daisy, following Jenny towards the bed.

'Very serious, Daisy.'

They watched and listened as Leo worked, and at the end he straightened up and gave Jenny an almost imperceptible nod. She listened as he explained to the young man that he was going to have to have another small operation. He managed to convey urgency without panic, and Jenny couldn't help but admire the way in which he set the boy's mind at ease without over-minimalising the dangers.

They moved outside the curtains. 'I'll get on to Theatre straight away,' he said. 'Can you bring me his drug chart? And I'll write him up for a pre-med. He'd better have that now—he's trying to hide it, but he's as anxious as hell.'

'Sure.'

By the time they had shipped Joe Lyons off to Theatre it was almost two-thirty, and the rest of Jenny's duty sped by as they attempted to catch up on the normal routine ward work which had had to be neglected to some degree during the emergency.

Joe was sent back to the ward from Recovery just before she went off duty, and she quickly read the operation notes. All seemed to have gone well. She took his blood-pressure and pulse, and counted his respirations. All were satisfactory.

She was just unpinning her cap in the office when Leo walked in—looking like a man who had spent the day on a battlefield. He brightened a little when he saw her cheerful expression.

'How's Joe Lyons?' he asked as he flopped into the nearest chair.

'He's absolutely fine!' she beamed. 'Limb nice and warm and pink, all his observations are spot on—looks like you did a magnificent job there!'

'Well, thanks,' he said in a bemused voice, as if reeling from her words of praise.

She realised that her hair had started to fall

down around her face, and furthermore that she was standing with her cap still in her hand, a foolish grin all over her face!

'I—er—I'd better get going,' she said quickly.

'Me, too. You know I won't be in tomorrow?'

'I didn't. No.'

'Oh, don't worry—I've arranged a locum cover. I'm taking my exam.' He began to write in Joe Lyons's notes.

'Leo?'

'Mm?' He glanced up at her, and in that moment when the dark brown eyes held her in their gaze she wished to high heaven that she had not been so dismissive with him when he had first arrived.

'Good luck for tomorrow.'

The wide smile was dazzling—she could see exactly why India Westwood had been so crestfallen!

'Thanks.'

And two days later he announced to the assembled nurses, who were just gathering together for the handover, that the paper hadn't been too bad, and he was obviously right because he was recalled to sit the viva the following week.

Jenny was just finishing the Kardex at the end of a busy day, during which she had wondered on more than one occasion how Leo's locum had passed his finals—let alone qualified as a surgeon—when Leo himself walked in, grinning happily, and she knew immediately that he'd been successful.

'You've passed!' she exclaimed, and for a

moment she thought that he was about to hug her, but he didn't, just giving another happy smile.

'I got a distinction!' he told her, trying without success to sound modest.

'Leo! That's wonderful.' Her delight was obviously genuine, and the brown eyes were regarding her thoughtfully.

'I must say—I thought so, too! Now, say after me, "Congratulations, Leo."'

His joy was infectious. 'Congratulations, Leo.'

'Now say, "I'd love to have dinner with you tonight."' His light-hearted tone hadn't changed, but the expression on his face was serious.

She could feel her heart thudding loudly in her chest. 'You haven't asked me,' she said, very quietly.

'If I ask you you'll only say no.'

'I might not.'

'You always do.'

She could feel her spirits soaring by the second. 'Isn't it a woman's prerogative to change her mind?' she teased him.

The deep voice became almost a whisper. 'Will you?'

'Yes,' she answered simply.

'I'll pick you up at eight.'

'Fine,' she smiled, and as she walked towards the door she felt about sixteen years old.

CHAPTER EIGHT

JENNY stood back from the mirror in her bedroom and eyed her reflection critically, wondering if she would do. She had been in a panic over what to wear, not knowing where Leo would take her.

In the end she had chosen to wear a flared white ballerina-length skirt, which set off her tiny waist to its best advantage, teamed with a ruffled white blouse of softest lawn. To break up the starkness of the white she wore a jade brooch, which echoed the green of her eyes, together with matching earrings.

When she answered the door punctually to him at eight, she knew from the expression on his face that she had chosen correctly.

Some men might have worn a suit for a first date, she mused, but Leo hadn't, and in point of fact she could never had imagined him in something so formal and conventional. But he looked very nice all the same, in a soft linen shirt of creamy beige, unbuttoned at the neck to reveal that he possessed a very brown chest indeed. The shirt was tucked into brown cords.

He saw her quick assessment. 'Will I do?' he teased her.

'Not bad,' she answered, trying without success to hide a smile.

'You look——' he began, and then apparently changed his mind, for his next words were quite different. 'I hope you don't mind staying in the village tonight. I had a feeling that you wouldn't be too keen to ride my motor bike——'

'You were right!' she interrupted vehemently.

'—and it didn't seem the right thing to do to ask to take your car, so we're stuck here! Do you mind?'

'Not at all,' she said, surprising even herself. It would be a very public date, but, strangely enough, she didn't seem to care.

'I've arranged a meal for us, to be served in the private room at the pub,' he said, looking very pleased with himself.

'How on earth did you manage that?'

He smiled. 'The landlord asked my advice about his gammy leg. I told him I'd see him in Out-patients—he obviously wants to keep on the right side of me! They serve good food in the pub—the room was his suggestion when I hinted that I wanted to go somewhere a little more private.'

They had begun to walk over the green, and she turned her head quickly on the pretence of check-ing her house, glad that he couldn't see her face. The trouble he'd gone to and his emphasis on the word 'private' made her aware of their closeness and what had happened on previous occasions when they had been alone together. Was she sure she could trust her feelings where he was concerned?

She felt even worse when they were ushered in

ceremoniously by Jack, the landlord, amid the interested smiles of the regular drinkers, and when they were settled with menus and gin and tonics she took a huge mouthful to try and quell her nerves—then nearly choked!

'I'm as nervous as you are,' he told her softly.

'Nervous!' she exclaimed indignantly. 'How do you know I'm nervous?'

He gave that crinkly smile. 'Well, if you continue to drink at that rate—I'll be carrying you out later! And, unless you're trying to practice your origami, there's no need to fold every napkin on the table!'

She looked down and saw that she had indeed pleated two of the pink napkins, and she started to laugh.

'That's better!' he said approvingly.

They were served with smoked-mackerel pâté to start.

'I was surprised you agreed to come,' he said, watching as she bit into a piece of brown bread. 'You don't hate me any more, then?'

She sighed as she put her knife down. 'I didn't really hate you, Leo—I over-reacted. Most of what you said made sense. I guess I was just being sensitive.'

'I'd never have made it into the diplomatic corps,' he admitted ruefully. 'It's a good thing I was better at sciences!'

'Do you realise that I know absolutely nothing about you?' she said suddenly.

'Other than what a brilliant surgeon I am?'

'And that modesty isn't one of your attributes!'

'What would you like to know?' he enquired as he tipped some Chablis into their glasses.

'Where you were born, where your parents live. That sort of thing.'

'Only if you promise to tell me about yourself afterwards.'

She smiled. 'That sounds fair enough.'

Leo gave her a rapid run-through. He was thirty-three. He had a brother called Louis who lived in London. Both his parents were alive and lived in London as well.

'My father is a merchant banker,' he explained, 'and he's very disappointed that neither son followed in his footsteps.'

'Didn't you fancy going into the City?' She smiled as she was served with a seafood platter.

'I hated it,' he said passionately after Jack had gone. 'All that time and energy spent in pursuing something as intrinsically worthless as money. They see me as a rebel! They keep hoping I'll come to my senses!'

'They don't like your being a doctor?' she asked incredulously.

'They think it's slave-labour,' he replied cheerfully. 'They could understand it if I were going to do lots of private work—but, of course, I'm against that.'

'Good,' she said in a low voice. Their eyes met and he smiled.

He drank some wine. 'Now it's your turn.'

'Mine isn't half as interesting,' she protested.

'You promised.'

'So I did.' She pushed her plate away. 'I've always lived here, in this village. On my own now, but with my mother until her death three years ago.'

His face grew soft with sympathy. 'And your father?' he probed.

She tried without success to quash the still-present feeling of hurt and betrayal. 'My father left us when I was four years old.'

'That must have been awful for you.'

For once she didn't try to be brave. She didn't feel she had to with him. 'It was pretty bad, but you get over it.'

'And your mother never married again?'

She shook her head. 'They never actually divorced—I don't know why. At one point I thought she seemed close to Harry Marlow, but nothing ever came of it.'

'I had no right to stop them from bringing you back for his funeral,' he said quietly. 'Can you forgive me for that?'

The sincerity of his apology wiped away any last traces of resentment. 'Of course I can. You did what you thought was best, and maybe it was best—I *did* need the holiday. I'd been working without a real break since Mummy died—perhaps that's why I'm so uptight.'

'You're not uptight,' he smiled.

'You said I was,' she argued, smiling back at him.

'Put it like this,' he told her. 'You don't look in the least bit uptight tonight.'

'I don't feel it,' she admitted. 'And I owe you an apology, too.'

He paused in the middle of buttering a piece of bread. 'How so?'

She smiled a little wryly. 'When you arrived and made all those changes, I rather hotheadedly accused you of driving Judy away. I know now that it isn't true. I received a letter from her. She said that she felt she was due for a change. She also said that she agreed with you about not recalling me for the funeral. I leapt to a lot of the wrong conclusions, and I'm sorry.'

'It doesn't matter,' he said softly and, reaching across the table, he took her hand in his. The dark eyes were tender in the subdued lighting of the room. It was the first time he had touched her all evening, and the air felt as if it had been sprinkled with magic, everything in the room seeming to sparkle and spangle, and Jenny was filled with an overwhelming desire to have him kiss her once more, to kiss her with all the passion and fervour that he had done once before, high on a wind-swept hill.

Then the door to the restaurant opened and Jack appeared with a tray to clear away the dishes, and the spell was broken. After that they chatted generally, but she was aware of a highly charged emotional undercurrent.

Afterwards she couldn't remember what she'd eaten or drunk, or even much of what they had spoken about; she was aware only of his smile and of a sense of expectation.

He walked her home, his hand resting lightly on her shoulder. Neither spoke, yet the silence was not constrained, and when they reached the door to her cottage she turned to him, expectant and nervous.

But the kiss, when it came, surprised her more than anything—the lightest touch of his lips to her cheek, so light that she might almost have dreamt it.

'It's been a wonderful evening, Jenny,' he said. 'Can we do it again tomorrow?'

'Yes—I'd—I'd love to,' she stuttered.

'Until tomorrow, then,' he whispered, and then he was gone, walking back over the green, turning just once to smile at her, and she let herself in the front door, unsure of whether she was more bemused, surprised or disappointed.

This pattern continued for the next week. They saw each other every night, except when he was on call. He even hired a car!

She couldn't believe it when he arrived to collect her in a shiny new saloon.

'Where did you get this?' she asked incredulously.

'I rented it.'

'But why?'

He sighed. 'I should have thought that was obvious, Sister Hughes! You won't ride on the back of my bike, will you?'

'No,' she said firmly.

'So, unless we spend every evening in the delightful yet undoubtedly limited venues which this village has to offer, we need some other form of transport!'

'But I've got a car!' she told him.

'And I'm being conventional for once,' he growled.

She couldn't believe just how proper he was being! He treated her as if she were a delicate piece of porcelain, and she began to wish that he wouldn't! She began to long for him to take her in his arms and kiss her properly.

Jenny discovered that they really *were* very different—he cared very little for material possessions. She couldn't understand why he had never bought a place of his own.

'Because I'm not ready to put down roots,' Leo had shrugged.

Perhaps that should have warned her, but she chose to ignore it.

She was the practical one—he was the visionary.

'I know that there's something I want to do,' he told her one evening. 'I just haven't found it yet.'

'Isn't it a little late for a change of direction?' she ventured.

'Jenny, darling, it's never too late.'

'We're so incompatible,' she sighed.

'Just different,' he teased. 'And, when all else fails, we'll compromise.'

His words unsettled her sometimes, yet he made her laugh as no one else had ever done, and so, in spite of the occasional vague misgiving, she continued to see him without allowing herself many thoughts on where they were heading.

The sixth time she went out with him he took her straight from work to see a film, and they ate popcorn and ice-cream and argued all the way back about whether the hero had been obtuse in not realising that the heroine had been in danger from his business partner.

They drove up the main street towards her house.

'Would you like me to cook you some supper?' he asked casually.

Her heart had started beating very, very fast. She was twenty-six, not sixteen, and she was extremely attracted to him. If she went home with him the outcome would be inevitable. She knew what perhaps she should say, and she knew what she wanted to say. 'I'd love some supper.'

He parked outside his cottage, and as he let her in she shivered.

'Leave your coat on until I light a fire,' he told her softly, and she complied, watching as he fiddled around with paper and firelighters until she realised that he was making absolutely no headway, and she took the matches from his hand.

'Here. Let me.' She deftly rearranged the logs and lit the paper, and soon there was a brilliant orange blaze crackling and spitting in the grate.

'You're a genius!' he declared, and she pretended to frown.

'Don't tell me you've only just discovered that?'

His hands had gone lightly to her shoulders, and the brown eyes were very serious. 'You know I love you, don't you?'

She didn't doubt his words for a moment—it had been something she had known all week. 'Yes, Leo.'

'Jenny. . .' he began, but the sentence was never finished because she was in his arms and he was kissing her. 'God, Jenny. . .' he muttered. 'I've been wanting to do this all week.' His mouth found hers again. 'I've never felt like this in my life before. I've been crazy for you, from the first time I saw you. I was like a love-struck schoolboy.' He kissed her again. 'I should have taken my time with you, instead of going hell for leather! I thought I'd blown it—I never thought I'd get another chance. I'm afraid to start kissing you again, because I don't know if I'll ever be able to stop, and that might not be what you want, my darling.'

But she *wanted* him to kiss her again, and she reached out for him, thinking that he would encircle her in that powerful embrace once more, but he did no such thing.

Without even touching her body, he began to brush his lips against hers, but so softly that she was sure that she had imagined it, and those little half-kisses were such sweet torment that soon she could bear it no longer and her arms went up around his neck, and she began to kiss him passionately.

She heard him chuckle, and somehow they had slid to the floor and become a heap of tangled limbs in front of the fire.

He looked at her steadily and she could see the firelight reflected in the deep, dark eyes.

'Are you sure this is what you want?'

She stared very hard at him. 'I'm sure.'

'Good,' he murmured. 'I've always wanted to make love in front of a roaring fire!'

And suddenly it became something she had always wanted to do, too. He began to kiss the slim pale column of her neck, and she sighed as he reached a particularly sensitive spot in the base of her collar-bone. Funny, she thought dreamily— she would have called it clavicle at work! He continued to kiss her, and then she wasn't thinking at all.

Vaguely she was aware that his hand had moved down to her shirt, and that he was slowly unbuttoning it, pushing the filmy fabric aside as he found the aching mound of her breast. She felt a mounting, burning excitement as first his hand, and then his mouth explored the sensitive skin there. For one dizzyingly wonderful moment she looked down to see his dark head on her chest.

She sighed his name as his hand moved down her body, and without thinking she began to unbutton his shirt.

Again she had that uncanny feeling of being at one with the elements, of merging with the earth and the wind and even the fire which illuminated their increasingly naked bodies.

For the briefest of moments their gaze held, and it was then that she knew with a heart-rending certainty that, unsuitable or not, she loved him too.

She awoke to find that Leo had one leg lying on top of hers and that they were both stark naked in his bed.

Disbelief flooded over Jenny as the events of the previous evening and night came flashing back to her. What had she done?

She'd let him make love to her with rapturous and enthusiastic response, first on the floor of his sitting-room, and then allowing him to lead her upstairs where they had gone to bed and spent most of the night doing variations of the same thing—that's what she'd done. Staid, dependable, sensible Jenny Hughes had thrown caution to the wind—and how! She let out a small groan.

'Let me guess.' The deep voice sounded highly amused. 'Sister Hughes is lying there, regretting everything that has happened and wishing herself a million miles away?' The brown eyes were shining with laughter as Leo propped himself up on an elbow and stroked an errant wisp of hair gently from her cheek.

She blushed at the evidence of his powerful nakedness, so clear in the bright spring sunshine which shone through the uncurtained windows they'd neither had the time nor the inclination to draw last night.

'I shouldn't be here!' she wailed.

'That's not what you said last night!' he grinned. Just what *had* she said last night? She could remember echoing his sighs of pleasure, of whispering endearments, even of choking little words as she'd begged him not to stop. . . She hastily closed her eyes as if by doing so she could blot out the vivid pictures her thoughts evoked. She'd never have dreamed that she could be so—so—uninhibited.

He had begun to kiss her shoulder, and instinctively she wriggled with pleasure.

'I don't want you to think. . .' she began.

'I'm not thinking very clearly at all at the moment,' he whispered.

'I'm not always doing this kind of thing. . .'

He smiled then. 'I don't care. I don't make value judgements like that, Jenny. It doesn't matter whether you've had one lover or millions!'

'Millions!' She glared.

'I'm joking, my darling. I love you. I care about you. Now come here.'

'I have to go——'

'Not yet, you're not. . .'

When he was like this he was irresistible. Common sense and straight thinking seemed to fly out of the window when she was in his arms. Her mind was telling her to go, and her body was resisting most strenuously. . .

'That was amazing,' he sighed, echoing her last conscious thoughts as they lay locked in each other's arms afterwards.

She had had one previous sexual experience. She'd gone out with a dental student for almost a year when she'd been training. She'd thought she'd been in love with him, and had deliberated for ages before going to bed with him. That had been a disaster, and she had realised quite soon after that she hadn't loved him at all.

And yet she had gone to bed so easily with Leo; there had been little real agonising about it. So did that mean she loved him? Last night she had thought she did.

'What are you dreaming about?' he enquired lazily.

'Nothing.' She sounded evasive, but he turned her head to face him.

'You can't keep secrets from me, Jenny. Don't you know I can read your mind?'

'You're in the wrong profession,' she laughed. 'You're so persuasive that you could have been a barrister!'

'I still could,' he said.

'Don't be ridiculous! You're a doctor.'

He caught her hand and kissed it. 'Today I'm a doctor, tomorrow and this year a doctor. But next year? Who knows? Maybe I'll sail around the world and take you with me!'

The hand that he held felt suddenly icy, as if a chill blanket had enveloped it, for his words sent alarm bells ringing inside her head. They reminded her of her first impressions of him—unconventional, off-beat, his hair just too long, his behaviour sometimes eccentric. It didn't matter that he was strong and kind and attractive if they were fundamentally unsuited. What was the point of falling in love with a man who was as unpredictable as he sounded?

He sensed the change in her. 'Now what's going on in that neat little head of yours?'

'I'm just thinking that I've never been late for work in my life,' she said lightly. 'And I'm not going to start now.'

'Let me take you in with me.'

'No!' she said firmly. Imagine the reaction if she turned up with him. The gossips would have a field-day!

'Oh, go on,' he repeated softly.

'No!'

She then had the embarrassment of pulling the rumpled sheet off the bed and wrapping it around herself like a Greek goddess. His eyes crinkled as he laughed at her discomfiture.

'Boiled egg and soldiers?' he asked hopefully.

'No chance!' she retorted, but he had leapt out of bed and taken her in his arms, and she had to pull away hastily, realising that they could be seen from the green.

'So much for my reputation!' she said crossly.

'Then I'll have to make an honest woman of you, won't I? Will you marry me, Jenny?'

For some reason this outraged her. 'Don't be so flippant, Leo! You can't offer marriage to someone you've just met, as though you were offering a plate of cakes! It can't be taken lightly—or aren't you aware that one in three marriages end in divorce?'

'Including your parents'?' he asked shrewdly.

'They didn't actually divorce.'

'In all but name they did. And you, of course, are determined not to replicate the mistakes of your parents?'

'Of course I'm not. If and when I decide to get married it will be after a lot of careful thought and consideration.'

'Not too much—I might not wait that long!'

'You are a conceited man, Leo Trentham, to think that I might be referring to you!'

He still had her pinned up against the wall, wrapped in a sheet, the tanned, craggy face very close to her own, the corners of the brown eyes crinkling.

She was trapped and enjoying it very much, and—what was more—he knew it. 'Are you going to let me go to work now?' she asked him.

'Only if you repeat what you told me last night,' he whispered, a devilish look on his face.

She had said many things to him last night, but she knew the one thing he wanted to hear. She was muddled and confused about so many things—whether or not she should have rushed so willingly into an affair with a man like him. Someone who was so unlike herself.

They argued, but he made her laugh. He was thirty-three and yet he didn't seem to know what he really wanted from life. He was everything she had once thought she despised in a man, and yet her feelings for him ran stronger than anything she had ever before experienced.

Yes, she was confused—but she knew one thing for sure. . .

'Yes, damn you, Leo Trentham,' she whispered softly, 'I love you, you know I do.'

CHAPTER NINE

So WHY wouldn't she agree to marry him?

'It's too soon,' she told him the second time he asked her. They were lying in bed and he was feeding her grapes.

'Aren't you supposed to peel them for me?' she giggled.

'Mm?'

'Leo! That one has trickled juice all over. . .'

'I'll lick it off,' he murmured.

'You're unbelievable!' she sighed.

'So are you! So why won't you marry me?'

'I told you—it's too soon. Why rush into it when we're having a perfectly good time as we are?'

'Typical,' he muttered. 'The one woman I *do* want to marry and she turns me down!'

'I suppose that hundreds of others would have leapt at the chance?' she asked indignantly.

'A few,' he agreed, smiling as he saw her glare.

'Then maybe it's just the fun of the chase you like?' she suggested. 'Perhaps as soon as I say yes you'll get cold feet.'

'Don't,' he warned her. 'Don't cheapen it. We love each other. A fact. Nothing can change that.'

Couldn't it? she wondered. Love did change— everyone knew that, or else why was the divorce rate so dramatically on the increase? Her own parents must have been madly in love with one another once, like this. Hard to believe, she knew, when she remembered the bitterness in her mother's voice whenever her father's name was mentioned.

'Don't throw your life away for a man,' she had warned her on more than one occasion. 'They're not worth it.'

Not that Leo was asking her to throw anything away, mind you. Although he steadfastly refused to discuss what they might do, or where they might live.

'We'll discuss the future when you've agreed to marry me,' he teased her.

'I can't believe that someone like you could be so conventional,' Jenny grumbled.

'And I can't believe that someone like you could be so *unconventional*,' he parried.

'If I were being really conventional, then I wouldn't be lying in bed with you like this,' she pointed out. 'And besides, most men would be delighted to find a woman who wasn't clamouring to get them up the aisle.'

'And I told you once before—I am not most men. All I want from you is your love.'

And love in Leo's eyes meant marriage. And marriage frightened the hell out of her.

In the meantime, life went on. They made no effort to keep their affair a secret, although they travelled to work separately, mostly because Leo was too stubborn to be driven by Jenny, and she was too scared to go on his bike. And neither would back down on the issue.

Only India Westwood had a slightly changed attitude towards her. The two women had never got on particularly well, but now it was worse. Whether or not it had anything to do with the fact that Jenny had witnessed Leo turning down India's invitation to a rock concert, Jenny didn't know, but there was a thinly veiled hostility from the staff nurse towards her ward sister once word got out about her and Leo.

A part of her felt reborn—she realised how long it had been since she had been part of a couple, and even when she had been out with people before it had never been like this. They spent every minute they could together. They discussed anything and everything, vociferously and passionately. Jenny felt no awkwardness or shyness or embarrassment when she was with him.

And the physical side just got better and better. Jenny sometimes felt that it was unfair to be going in to work feeling this way, her cheeks glowing, her eyes shining, remembering something he had said, something he had done.

While at work he was the model of deference towards her. Indeed, sometimes she thought that she might have imagined being in bed with him the night before, since nothing in his manner betrayed any evidence of the new intimacy between them.

And then the snows came. Unseasonal late-March blizzards, the likes of which had not been seen since the end of the last century. Things were so bad that many of the access roads to and from the hospital began to look in danger of being blocked, so all staff who could were asked to stay on hospital premises until the inclement weather had passed.

'They've given me a room in the nurses' home,' Jenny told Leo as they drank their afternoon tea together in the canteen.

'Well, you won't be using it—you can stay with me in the doctor's mess—the rooms are bound to be far bigger.'

'Do you think they'd mind?'

"They? Just who are "they"?'

She shrugged. 'The admin.'

'Jenny,' he took her hand and smiled, 'I don't care what they think. You're a nurse—not a nun. You've already taken the vows of poverty and obedience—there's no need to throw in chastity too!'

There was something illicit and wonderful about lying together on the narrow hospital bed. It was anonymous, like being in a cheap hotel in a foreign country. There was nothing to do but lie in one another's arms for hours, to talk, and doze, and make love again.

Until the night of the storm.

The first they knew was the report from the radio. Telegraph poles were down, there were great drifts concealing treacherous drops down the icy mountain roads. Motorists were advised not to leave home unless their journey was absolutely vital.

'No emergency admissions tonight, then,' said Leo.

'We *hope*,' said Jenny, unpinning her hair. She had been on a late duty. The ward had been half empty and very quiet. Four routine cases hadn't been able to get into the hospital, and had been cancelled until the weather improved. It was almost midnight, and they were sitting in Leo's room. He had just finished making some notes from a textbook, and they were clearing these away to eat some sandwiches when the phone beside the bed rang.

She heard only a series of brief responses from Leo, and she could see from the tension on his face that it was serious.

'What?' she mouthed at him, but he shook his head.

'She's here, actually,' he said into the mouth-piece. 'I'll put it to her, and then I'll ring you back.'

He put the phone down and went directly over to her, crouching by her feet, taking both hands into his.

'Listen to what I say very carefully, my darling. There's been a very bad accident out on the Glower Road—a farmer who was trying to rescue an injured sheep has been hit by a falling boulder and he's trapped. Visibility is poor—the air-rescue plane can't get near him and they think that too much of the road has been blocked up for an ambulance or four-wheel drive to get through. They need an experienced surgeon right away and I'm going. If I have to operate I'll need a nurse with me, and I want you. The problem is that I'm going to have to take the bike.'

'But I haven't worked in Theatre for years!' she protested.

'You're orthopaedically trained,' he insisted. 'There's no one here with your experience. It'll all come back to you. I need you, Jenny, but I don't want to force you on to the bike—I know how you feel about them. The decision is yours.'

The moment was long enough for her to register the concern in his eyes, to see the apprehension written into the deep laughter-lines around his mouth, and to note that the adrenalin which had begun to pump around his body in readiness had caused a muscle in the side of his cheek to work furiously.

Her fear of motor bikes had been with her for years. She had seen more tragedy and damage done by them as an orthopaedic nurse than by anything else. She would have banned them if she could.

But she loved Leo, and he needed her help. The question was, did she trust him enough to put away her fear just for this one night? She knew there could only be one answer.

She swallowed. 'I'll come,' she told him.

There was a brief, grateful smile. 'Let's go, then.'

He made her don layers of warm clothing, a thermal vest, a T-shirt, thick sweater and her own tracksuit trousers. Over these she wore water-proofs—far too long, and needing to be turned up at the bottoms. He gave her a muffler, fur-lined leather gloves and a helmet to carry.

Someone had brought his bike round to Casualty and there were people milling around. Leo was given an emergency pack which contained pain relief, entonox gas and an operation kit.

Sonia Walker, the nursing officer, was there. 'Are you sure you'll be all right, Jenny?'

Jenny managed a smile. 'I'm not sure at all, Sonia—all I can do is hope, and do whatever Leo tells me.'

He had climbed on to the front of the powerful machine. The constant whine and howl of the wind made his words to her curiously disembodied.

'Are you ready, honey?'

She climbed on the back behind him, clasping him as tightly as she could, her nervousness tempered slightly by the endearment, which he would not normally have used at work.

She had never been on a motor bike before, and the furious roar as he revved up was enough to make her shiver, but there was no time for doubt or second thoughts, for he had accelerated and was speeding down the drive and out of the gates, with the cold wind whipping like a coil against her cheeks.

Afterwards she could remember little of the drive—the fear had driven normal responses from her body. Instead of staring aghast at the precipitous drops, or shuddering at the small sharp swerves that Leo made when his powerful headlights illuminated yet another fallen obstacle, she simply welded her body close to his, mainly for relief from cold, but partly from the comfort she derived from knowing that he was there.

Once she thought she heard him shout to her, but she couldn't be sure, and she could think of nothing that he might be asking other than if she was OK, and so for an answer she gave him a squeeze.

Just keeping still on the machine and making sure that she leaned the same way as he did was enough to occupy her thoughts, and even if it hadn't been she wouldn't have dared to dwell on whether she and Leo might ever again lie together in the narrow hospital bed. She didn't for a moment minimise the danger to themselves.

Leo had been given instructions as to where the man lay—left just before the turning into Blencowe Farm, past a dip and a hollow in the side of the road where the sheep sometimes sheltered on their journey to the fields of the farm.

The first thing they saw was the dead sheep— the animal which Jeff Farlow had inadvertently risked his life for now lay inert and lifeless, the white coat becoming steadily whiter as the small flurries of snow fell and settled.

Leo pulled to a halt at the same time as a tall, burly figure materialised from the side of a massive boulder, and Jenny recognised the figure of

Farlow's son. In the hazy light the boy's face looked even whiter than the coat of the sheep.

'Where is he?' demanded Leo briefly.

'Over here.'

He led the way to the far side of the giant, brooding rock, and Leo crouched down and flashed the strong light of the torch on to the man's face. Jenny could immediately see that he was in shock.

Leo stood up and began to assess the extent of the damage, while Jenny located a very weak and extremely rapid pulse. She pulled a metal 'space blanket' from her pack and gingerly began to wrap it around his shoulders.

Leo came back, his face grim. 'The lower end of his left leg is completely trapped by the rock. There's no way that I can save it. Even if we had enough men here to shift the rock, the leg is irreparably damaged. I'm going to have to amputate.'

She could see the Farlow son blanch. Leo's words had been brusque and to the point, but here, when every one of them was in danger, there was no time to attempt to couch the bad news in anything less than totally frank terms.

'I'm going to need help,' said Leo. 'People to hold lights—that kind of thing. Is there anyone else up at the house?'

'My brother.'

'Can you fetch him now?'

The man nodded and sped off. Leo turned to Jenny. 'We'd better treat the shock before we take the limb off. Can you draw up twenty milligrams of morphine? I'm going to find a vein, and then we'll whack in a few litres of plasma expander.'

Jenny drew up the powerful painkiller with hands which were trying not to shake. It was absolutely freezing without her gloves on. Meanwhile Leo was slapping at the man's arm, trying without success to find a vein. Jenny could see an unaccustomed desperation worn into the strong features, knowing that precious seconds were ticking by.

'Got it!' he exclaimed, and held his hand out for the cannula she had ready.

He rapidly injected the drug, and then followed this up with two litres of haemocel, all the time speaking quietly to the patient, though Jenny doubted whether he actually heard anything.

Leo looked up. 'Can you remember the procedure for emergency amputation?'

She'd read about it, of course, but a long time ago, almost as long ago as when she'd last assisted in an operation. . .

'It's pretty basic, isn't it?'

He nodded. 'Very. I'll just yell for what I want. Don't take it personally.'

'Don't worry. I won't.'

The two men arrived, gasping for breath. Jenny pulled out some gloves and put the instruments on a sterile towel. Three other large towels she used to surround the limb—she knew that it would be impossible for the operation to be conducted aseptically but she wanted to minimise the risk of infection as much as she could.

Leo was shouting instructions, arranging for the strong torches to be held where they could best aid him.

'This isn't going to be a pretty sight,' he said grimly. 'But I don't need any more casualties on my hands. Do you think you're both up to it?' He looked directly at the two men, seeing the fear of the unknown written in their eyes.

The older one nodded. 'Carry on, Doctor. We'll be all right.'

It was not a pretty sight, and even someone as experienced as Jenny could not help blanching as Leo began to use the circular saw. . .

She passed instruments back and forth to him, responding immediately to his curt demands, putting up yet more haemocel at his instruction. Speed was of the essence and he worked fast, but the line of the amputation was as neat as any she'd seen. The limb came away and she wrapped it in another towel. She saw the youngest of the men turn his face away.

Leo began roughly sewing up the skin flaps. 'He'll have to go back to Theatre for tidying up when he recovers,' he said.

If he recovers, thought Jenny.

The only sounds were of Leo working and the chill wind whistling around them. Once the silence was broken by the sound of a distant rock tumbling down the side of the mountain, and Leo looked up, startled.

'God,' he muttered. 'That's all we need.'

But there was nothing more. Leo finished

sewing up. 'We can't leave him here,' he said flatly. 'We're going to have to carry him to the house. Jenny, you take care of his head and his airway? I'll take the wound site. You two are going to have to look after the rest. We have got to be quick, but careful. Is that understood?'

'Yes,' they all replied in unison.

Somehow—she never knew how they did it—they struggled with the inert form back to the house, the wind howling around them. Jenny had been terribly afraid that Jeff Farlow would die in transit. but he was a big strong man, and when his wife opened the door to them she burst into floods of tears.

'Oh, Jeff,' she sobbed. 'Oh, my God—thank God he's safe!'

'I need a space cleared on the floor. Quickly!' barked Leo.

The urgency of this communication seemed to bring Mrs Farlow to her senses, and she hastily pushed aside sofas and chairs so that at last they could lay him on the floor.

Jenny and Leo gently manoeuvred him into a recovery position, extending his airway as much as possible.

Afterwards they were told that they spent four hours in that room, Jenny continuing to squeeze in plasma expander, and Leo, at one point, having to resuture part of the stump of the amputated limb.

She remembered being given tea to drink and

wincing slightly at the disproportionate amount of sugar which had been piled in.

'Drink it, darling,' she remembered Leo saying to her and had worried what the Farlow family might think of the endearment, but no one had appeared to notice.

Neither of them noticed the wind drop or the pale light of dawn as it began to penetrate the room.

Then Leo looked up suddenly. 'Listen!'

They listened. Jenny at first thought he'd imagined something, but then, very faintly, she heard the familiar whirring of a propeller.

'They've sent someone,' she said weakly.

Leo smiled for the first time. 'They certainly have! It's the air ambulance, Mrs Farlow—we'll be able to get your husband to hospital now!'

Jenny thought that Mrs Farlow was about to throw her arms around the dark surgeon, but she obviously thought better of it. The whirring sound was getting closer and closer.

'Turn every light in the house on,' ordered Leo. 'And get those curtains back.'

Jenny stayed with the patient while Leo stood up and threw open the front door. She could hear the sound of the helicopter hovering.

They brought the craft down several hundred yards away from the house, and Jenny saw two crew descend immediately, clutching at a stretcher. A man and a woman followed; Jenny could tell from their clothing that one was a doctor and the other a nurse, but she didn't know them—they would have come from the city hospital.

She listened while Leo curtly recounted what had happened, numbly handing over the observation chart, which Jenny had drawn up, to the nurse.

'The weather's too dicey to take him far,' said the doctor. 'We're going to have to take him into Denbury.' He glanced at them. 'That's where you two are from, isn't it?'

'Yes,' said Jenny, nodding.

Two of the crew were easing him on to the stretcher. 'Do you want to accompany him,' one asked, 'or wait until the road clears?'

'We'll come,' said Leo briefly.

Jenny had never been in a helicopter before. It was deafeningly loud, but she was less frightened than she had imagined, considering that she had never even been on a plane before. The relief doctor and nurse had taken over the care of Mr Farlow, and Jenny and Leo sat squeezed together, with her holding tightly on to his hand.

'Someone will have to collect the amputated limb,' said Leo tiredly. 'And my bike.'

They landed at the front of the hospital, with the patient being lifted out carefully first, and when Jenny finally followed Leo down she had never seen so many people. She saw Sonia Walker busy organising nurses, and several other doctors also stood around.

Leo put his arm around her shoulder, and she leaned against him for support, exhausted now.

She cleared her throat. 'I hate motor bikes and they terrify me, but you drove very carefully and you made me feel safe. Thank you.'

He smiled. 'I haven't for a moment underestimated the courage it must have taken for you to come there with me tonight, and I love you for it.'

She raised her face to his and saw such a look of love there that she knew instantly that all her doubts had been foolish.

'What?' he said quietly.

'I love you, too,' she answered.

'I know that!' The dark eyes glinted.

'I want to marry you, Leo.'

They glinted even more. 'Do you, now? Was that a proposal?'

She laughed. 'I suppose it was. Will you?'

'Will I what?' he teased.

'Marry me!'

He bent his head close to her ear. 'Ask me later,' he whispered. 'When I'm in a more responsive mood.'

She blushed a deep pink.

'I suppose I'd better go and write up my notes,' he said. 'I'll have to take him up to Theatre in a few hours anyway.'

'I'll come with you,' said Jenny. 'I'd like to see him settled on the ward.'

They began to walk towards the main portals. The old stone glittered in the early-morning light, and Jenny didn't see the patch of ice until her foot was on it and she began to slip. Leo's arm was around her waist and he moved to catch her, but he moved awkwardly and before Jenny could realise what had happened he had fallen, his head striking one of the portals, his arm moving out as he tried to break his fall.

'Leo!' she screamed, but it was too late, and she scrambled down to him and cupped his head in her hands, because Leo, her strong, wonderful Leo, was lying unconscious in the snow.

CHAPTER TEN

HE was the worst patient she had ever had.

'Sister?'

Jenny looked up from the Kardex she'd been writing. 'Yes, Nurse?'

Daisy Galloway shifted uncomfortably from one foot to another. 'It's—er—it's Dr Trentham, Sister.'

'Yes, Daisy. And what is it this time?'

Daisy was filled with an uncontrollable urge to giggle so that she made a strange gulping sound. 'He's demanding a bed-bath, Sister, and he's insisting that you give it to him!'

That did it! She marched down to his cubicle— she'd put him as far away from her office as she could—and pulled back the curtain to find Leo leaning back on his pillows, wearing the blue pyjamas which she'd had to go out and buy specially, as he hadn't possessed a pair, and grinning devilishly at her. It took a monumental effort, but she looked at him sternly.

'That,' she said, 'was not funny.'

'What?' he enquired innocently.

'Sending young Daisy Galloway to ask me to bed-bath you! You're perfectly capable of washing yourself—and, even if you *did* need a bed-bath, I'd be the last person to do it!'

'But my arm hurts, Sister!' he wailed.

'Then I'll get Nurse to give you some analgesia,' she said briskly.

'Jenny, darling——'

'Don't "darling" me,' she spat.

'You haven't been near me since I came in here,' he protested.

He looked absolutely gorgeous lying there, she thought. 'Of course I haven't, you idiot! I can hardly nurse my lover, now, can I?'

'Fiancé,' he corrected.

'Fiancé,' she smiled.

He tried the winsome look which had been having such a good effect on every nurse on the ward. 'I don't see why not!'

'Leo Trentham,' she said primly, her mouth twitching at the corners, 'can you just imagine me giving you a bed-bath?'

'I certainly can,' he grinned. 'I've been fantasising about it ever since they brought me in here!'

She went pink, terrified that one of the nurses might be listening!

'I'll get Nurse Galloway to bring you a bowl right away,' she said sternly. 'And don't forget—you've only fractured your humerus.'

'Who's humerus?' he quipped.

'Ha ha!' she grinned, and left him.

Thank goodness he was being discharged tomorrow—the nurses spent every available moment running to see if he needed anything!

Leo had only been admitted with the fracture because he'd been concussed and they had wanted to observe him. Her mind went back to the terror she'd experienced as he'd lain inert in her arms. Like a replay of a film she recalled hearing herself scream, of staff running over to them, and of someone gently moving her away. . .

Daisy saw the look of concern on Sister's face. 'Is everything all right, Sister?'

Jenny smiled, the memory clearing. 'Take no notice of Leo, Daisy. He's going home tomorrow.' To my home, she thought. Our home now. 'I've never known a man make such a meal out of a broken arm!'

'It was lucky he didn't break his right arm, wasn't it, Sister?' asked Daisy eagerly. 'Or it might have affected his operating, mightn't it?'

'It might have done. But yes, he was lucky.' Lucky that the head injury hadn't been more serious and that he'd come round in a matter of minutes. Lucky. He had been lucky, but then, so had she. Lucky to have found him.

They had it all worked out. He would move in with her. A locum had been arranged for the six or seven weeks before his arm had mended.

'But what will you do all day?' she had asked him.

'Write papers, of course.' He grinned. 'And work out inventive ways of how I can make love to you with one arm in plaster!'

'Leo!'

Things were quite perfect. She had never been so happy. She sped off to work each morning in her little car, leaving Leo at home with his textbooks.

'It's actually bloody impossible to do loads of things,' he complained. 'Like tie shoelaces, or chop an onion. I feel guilty because I don't have a wonderful meal waiting for you every night.'

'It doesn't matter, you do the shopping—that's enough!'

They grew very close in the time it took his arm to heal. Jeff Farlow was mending nicely. Leo kept wanting to talk about the night of the accident.

'I felt—oh, it sounds crazy,' he explained. 'When I was out there operating—I felt really *alive*. As though the work I was doing was really important.'

'The work you do here in the hospital is really important,' she pointed out.

'It's not the same, Jenny. I felt that this mattered more. Didn't you feel that?'

'Not at all,' she said lightly, her smile betraying nothing of the irrational feeling of apprehension which his words provoked. Things were perfect just the way they were.

On one or two occasions, when they had eaten supper and sat before the fire they often lit if the evening was cold enough to warrant it, she noticed that he had begun to lapse into a preoccupied silence.

'What's making you frown so deeply?' she asked him one evening.

'Just thinking.'

'About. . .?'

He tenderly brushed a lock of hair away from her neck, and kissed it. 'The future. Us. Wondering where we'll end up living.'

'What's wrong with here?' she demanded in some alarm.

'Nothing, my darling. Nothing at all. But my job here doesn't last for ever. Sooner or later I'm going to have to look around for something else. You know that.'

She couldn't imagine living anywhere else. She'd spent her whole life in this village, and most of it in this small cottage. It had been the one secure fixture in her existence.

He took her to meet his parents, and she couldn't help but be impressed by the large elegant house in Holland Park. They stayed the night, albeit in separate beds, and on the drive home the following morning he was unusually snappy.

'What was all that stuff you and my mother were discussing last night?'

'Just weddings.'

'I could have sworn I heard someone mention "marquee".'

She had hoped to broach this later. 'Your mother thought it would be nice if we got married in London, and held the reception there. . .'

'Go on,' he said in an odd voice.

'It makes sense, doesn't it? I've no family, and we've not really got the room to have it at the cottage. They're dying to do it, Leo—it would mean so much to them——'

'No!' he said, so savagely that she saw his

knuckles whiten on the steering-wheel of the car. 'I'm not doing it, Jenny, and that's final! I won't be got up like some performing animal at a circus just to fulfil my mother's social expectations. Listen——' he had pulled over into a lay-by, and turned to her '—do you really want that kind of a wedding?'

She could see the pleading look in his eyes, and the vision she had been nursing all night of a grand occasion retreated just like the illusion it always had been.

'Of course I don't,' she smiled. 'Your mother is even more persuasive than you are, and that's saying something! Now move over and let me drive—I'm not sure that you should be using that arm so much.'

'Yes, Sister!' he said meekly.

And in bed that night they decided to have a simple church service, with a small reception at the pub afterwards.

'When?' she asked.

'When I find a job?' he suggested.

Leo began scouring the pages of the BMJ for jobs. He wrote his CV, and one of the secretaries from the hospital typed it for him. He brought it home for Jenny to read.

'Looks impressive,' she smiled up at him. 'You shouldn't have any problem finding a job.' She wasn't looking forward to moving to a strange new town where she knew no one, and his job was likely to be busy, leaving her to her own devices for much of the time. But she quelled her doubts, thinking them natural, but futile.

Then they had a tragic episode on the ward. A young man named Philip Simms, aged twenty-one, was admitted as an emergency. He had been involved in a motor-cycle accident and had sustained a fracture to his tibia. Leo operated on him, and the outcome was successful—and within two days Phil was sitting up in bed, winning over the hearts of the nurses and keeping the rest of the ward in stitches with his constant stream of puns and jokes.

It was the quiet period after lunch, most of the patients were gently snoozing on their beds, and Jenny was walking round the ward, checking that all the fluid and TPR charts were up to date before Leo arrived to do a quick ward round.

He arrived, still wearing his Theatre greens under his white coat, and gave her an affectionate grin.

'How would you like to go out to supper tonight?' he asked quietly.

'Love to!' she murmured, wishing for a moment that they weren't in the middle of the ward and she could throw her arms around his neck and give him an enormous kiss.

'Good. I'll book it. Now, then,' he said in a slightly louder and more formal voice. 'How are all my patients doing?'

They went from bed to bed. Leo discontinued a course of antibiotics on one patient, and started another patient on heparin. They got to Philip's bed. His bed was covered in motor-cycle maga-zines. Jenny made a soft clicking noise with her lips.

'You're making my ward look untidy!' she chided him laughingly. 'One magazine at a time! How many times do I have to tell you that? And I wish you'd read something other than these—hasn't your accident put you off for life?'

'You must be joking, Sister! I can't wait to be out of here so that I can do a ton-up on the motorway!'

'Don't take any notice of her, Phil,' butted in Leo. 'I've only managed to get her on the back of my bike once—I drove like an angel, and still she refuses to ride pillion!'

Jenny blushed. She knew that all the patients knew they were going out together—but Leo was so open about it!

'Have you got a bike, then, Doctor?' he asked interestedly.

'Sure have. . .'

Then followed a short discourse on the relative merits of Norton versus Honda, none of which Jenny understood—they might as well have been speaking in Dutch! Eventually she managed to drag Leo away and on to the next bed.

They were halfway down the beds on the other side when they heard a kind of strangled cry, so strange and so horrible that they both whirled round immediately. It was Philip; his hand was gripping at his neck convulsively and his lips were blue. Jenny and Leo flew over to his bed in an instant, and by the time they got there he was dead.

They went through all the motions of resuscitation. Jenny ran for the crash trolley and yelled to Daisy Galloway to put out the call for the team. She dragged the trolley back down to the bed, and pulled the curtains round. Leo rammed the crash board underneath the mattress to provide a firm base for the external cardiac massage he was rhythmically applying. A deathly hush had fallen over the ward.

Jenny took over the cardiac massage while Leo pulled out the instruments for intubation, but then the anaesthetist arrived and quickly intubated him while Leo put the chest leads on and fixed up the monitor. They worked in silence punctuated only by the sounds of their own heavy breathing or muttered instructions. But in her heart Jenny knew it was no good.

They tried everything—shocking him when the screen showed ventricular fibrillation, and even injecting adrenalin straight into the muscle of the heart when the tracing slowed down to the depressingly straight line of asystole.

Eventually Leo straightened up, his face grave. 'I think we've lost him,' he said finally, and the anaesthetist nodded.

Jenny and Daisy then had the even more depressing task of disconnecting all the equipment from the body, all the time with the face of the dead young man haunting them. Daisy was crying openly, and Jenny didn't attempt to stop her—she felt thoroughly shaken herself. She simply couldn't believe that he was gone—so young and so vital one minute, and the next. . .

A pulmonary or a fat embolus, she thought to herself; fat, most probably—always a risk with large-bone injuries—but the post-mortem would tell them exactly.

It was impossible for the ward to be anything but gloomy after that. Jenny and Daisy laid the body out, and all the curtains around the other patients' beds were drawn until the mortuary trolley had removed the mortal remains of Philip Simms.

Jenny sent Daisy off early—the girl was too upset to work—but Jenny was shocked to see Leo in the office, standing at the window, staring sightlessly at the trees bending to the wind, his face ashen beneath the tanned craggy features.

She wanted to go to him, to put her hand on the arm which was so stiff with tension, but of course she couldn't. Jackie Graham was waiting for her to hand over.

They had driven in together that morning, but when Jenny had him bleeped to find out how long he would be he sounded distracted.

'Don't bother waiting—I'm likely to be here for at least an hour. I'll see you later.'

She had never heard him sound so preoccupied. 'And what about supper—do you still want to go out?'

There was a slight pause. 'I don't think I do. Would you mind terribly?'

'No, of course not. I'll see you at home later. How will you get back?'

'I'll manage. I must go, darling—I have to scrub.'

His use of the word 'darling' reassured her briefly, yet she continued to experience a vague feeling of disquiet which would not shift.

At home she showered and changed, lit the fire and prepared a fresh tomato sauce to accompany the tagliatelle, but the minutes ticked by and still Leo didn't come. By nine-fifteen she was just contemplating cooking pasta just for herself, although her appetite seemed to have deserted her, when she heard his key in the lock and turned round to face him.

'You're late!' she accused before she could stop herself, and he crossed the room and pulled her into his arms. 'And you've been drinking!' Now what had made her sound like a character from a second-rate sit-com?

He sighed. 'I had two very large whiskies with my anaesthetist.'

'Who?'

'Andy McClaren.'

The same anaesthetist who had tried to resuscitate Philip Simms.

'Then how did you get home if you'd both been drinking?'

'For God's sake, Jenny!' he said exasperatedly. 'What is this? The Spanish Inquisition?'

'I'm sorry you feel that way,' she said stiffly.

'Listen.' He put his hands on her shoulders and

bent his head to hers. 'Alison Banbury gave me a lift home, if you must know.'

Alison Banbury. Staff nurse from Theatres. Buxom and brash, with a reputation for eating housemen for breakfast.

'Really?' she asked in a sarcastically formal tone. 'How nice for you!'

'Jenny, Jenny,' he said placatingly, 'surely you're not jealous of Alison Banbury? It's you I love, you idiot!'

'Then why didn't you come home and have two large whiskies with me?' she demanded.

'Because I wasn't planning to have a drink, because I didn't even know I wanted one until Andy gave it to me. Because I was so bloody impotent to help that boy today—that young boy.' His voice choked a little on the word. 'His life was over—just like that!' He snapped his fingers. 'And it could have been me, Jenny. Or you. Any day— it could all be over for any of us.'

So that was it. It hit every member of the hospital staff at some time or another, some later than others—they saw so much death that it was inevitable, really. At some time or other each and every one would relate to a patient who would not make it. The evidence of how tenuous was their hold on mortality would chill each one of them at some time. She was just surprised that Leo had gone for so long in his job without having experienced it before.

She took him in her arms and hugged him tenderly, and made him sit before the fire while she brought him supper. She didn't feel like cooking the pasta now, and instead she brought in a platter of cheeses and crackers and some fruit, but neither of them ate much and Leo drank most of the bottle of wine they opened.

She'd never seen him slightly drunk before, and he held her tightly in bed before falling into a deep sleep, but she lay there for ages afterwards, staring at the shadows on the ceiling, wishing that she could quash her feelings of resentment—that he had chosen to confide in Andy McClaren and Alison Banbury.

And not in her.

CHAPTER ELEVEN

THINGS got back to normal, or at least they seemed to, but Jenny quickly became aware that Leo had changed, that the incident had had a profound effect on him. She began to experience the negative sides of love—the fear of rejection and the feelings of irritation that things were not as rosy as they had been. She wasn't sure whether or not she was imagining it, but she felt that their initial closeness had disappeared, as if a gulf had appeared, and she couldn't bring herself to discuss it for fear that Leo might say that he no longer loved her.

On the surface everything was as it had been— they ate, and talked, and made love. But it was not the same.

Leo was restless. He began to take solitary walks over the hills, and Jenny was sure that she was losing him. One afternoon she tried to have him bleeped—only to be told that he was out of the hospital for the afternoon.

'Dr Boyden is covering for him,' said the operator. 'Would you like to speak to him?'

'Er—no, thank you,' said Jenny quickly. 'I'll leave it.'

She replaced the receiver quickly, feeling somehow hurt and cheated. At one time he would have told her if he wasn't going to be around. And where had he gone? For one wild and crazy moment she almost lifted the receiver again to check whether Alison Banbury was also out for the afternoon, until common sense reasserted itself. Jealousy was not a quality she had ever admired, and Leo had never given her any cause to be jealous.

She was on a late duty, and after she had handed over to the night staff she went and changed, and was walking along the corridor when a figure emerged from the shadows. It was Leo.

'You startled me!' she exclaimed, wondering why he was looking so smart. 'Where have you been?'

'I'll tell you when we get home' he promised.

By now they were in the darkness of the car park, and he pulled her into his arms and began to kiss her with hot, feverish kisses. She sighed with pleasure—he hadn't kissed her quite like that for weeks.

He raised his head and looked at her intently, and his dark eyes looked almost like jet. 'I've been unbearable these past few weeks,' he said. 'I must have been awful to live with. I'm sorry.'

Just the fact that he had acknowledged the friction made her feel immeasurably better, and she smiled. 'You can make it up to me,' she told him.

'Oh, I will,' he said.

He wanted to drive home, and she climbed into

the passenger-seat. A fine rain had begun to fall and he switched on the windscreen wipers so that they performed their monotonous swish-swish routine. She waited until they were out of the hospital grounds.

'So what's the big secret?' she asked.

'Let's wait until we get home. I don't want to have a car conversation. I want to see your face when I tell you.'

Tell me what? she wondered, but contented herself with waiting as the car swept homewards.

When they reached the cottage he insisted on lighting a fire as the night was so cold. He grinned as the coals began to glow orange.

'You taught me to light a fire, you know.'

'You've taught me a lot in return.' She dimpled and he started to kiss her.

'How would you feel about getting married in a month's time?' he whispered.

She drew back. 'I thought we agreed to wait until you'd found a job?'

'I have! It's the last. . . Oh, heck—I'm jumping the gun! I don't know where to begin.'

'Try at the beginning,' she suggested.

'The joint board of St Martin's and Denbury Hospital asked to see me this morning,' he said. 'They'd heard rumours that I was applying for jobs elsewhere.'

'Not guilty,' said Jenny. 'I haven't told a soul!'

'Well, you know what hospital grapevines are like! I expect the secretary told one of the other secretaries, and so on. And anyway, it doesn't matter that they did—they would expect me to be changing jobs now that I've got my fellowship.'

'And we keep calling you "Doctor" instead of "Mister",' teased Jenny. 'I must try to remember in future! So why did the board want to see you?'

'To offer me a job. Senior registrar based at St Martin's, but with responsibility for Denbury, too. And with some very strong hints that the consultancy could be mine in four years when Mr Elliott retires.'

'Leo! That's marvellous! They must really like you.'

He shrugged modestly. 'They said that they were very happy with my work.'

She looked at him closely. 'What's the matter? You don't sound very pleased.'

'I was flattered.'

'Flattered! I should think so, too! When do you start?'

'I'm not going to accept, Jenny,' he said quietly.

For a moment she thought that she hadn't heard him properly. 'What?'

'I'm not going to accept it.'

There was a short silence. 'What on earth are you talking about, Leo? It's a marvellous opportunity. You like the hospitals, you like the work. . . You told me that. And just think what a young consultant you'd be!'

'Let me tell you where else I've been today.'

She bit her lip in frustration. 'I can hardly wait.'

'I went to see the VSO today.'

'The who?'

'The Voluntary Services Overseas. They recruit medical and nursing staff to go and work in the Third World. Jenny, they need good doctors. And nurses. They're crying out for them. They could offer us both work. We could be married and out there in just over the month. Jenny, they *need* people like us.'

There was a recklessness about him which frightened her. Her stable future was threatening to disintegrate. She took a deep breath and forced herself to remain calm. 'They need us here, too,' she said, but he shook his head.

'I know that all medical care is valuable, but out there we'll be dealing with basic deprivation on a huge scale. Malnutrition and poor sanitation. And we can help educate—encourage mothers to breast-feed their babies instead of mixing powdered milk with water which as often as not is contaminated.' His eyes were ablaze with passion. 'Can't you see, Jenny?'

Her hair, still in the pleat she had worn for work, had begun to fall around her face. 'No, I can't, Leo. I can't see why you've had this sudden change of heart. Two weeks ago you were applying for surgical posts, and now you want to take a completely different course. What's brought all this on?'

He took her hand in his, but she let it lie there inert. 'I've been feeling like this for weeks now. It started with the accident in the snow, when I did the amputation. I felt more vital then than I'd ever done—that I'd helped save Jeff Farlow's life, and that I was young enough to do basic surgery, that I didn't need to be cosseted in the formal setting of a hospital. I won't be able to do work like that when I'm sixty, Jenny—that's why I want to do it *now*. I've been given a marvellous training and now I'd like to use it to benefit a nation of people who haven't been as fortunate as we have.'

She was shaking her head. 'I can't understand why you're saying all this.'

'Then I'll tell you.'

She could hear the conviction in his voice, see it blazing in the dark eyes.

'Do you remember that film we saw recently? Where the main character kept saying "*carpe diem*"—"seize the day"?'

'Yes, of course I do.'

'I looked at Philip Simms the other week, lying dead, and it frightened me to think that I could spend my whole life conforming to some nebulous plan which I hadn't really thought out, and that at the end of my life I could say that I hadn't really lived as I wanted to. I wanted to seize my day, and I want you with me. Even if we only do it for two years, think of the good we can achieve!'

'I can't believe this!' Her voice rose as she struggled to hide her anger. 'You've been given the chance of a lifetime. Promises of consultancy don't fall into your lap every day of the week. And you're turning it down! You want to take off to some God-forsaken part of the world, and you expect me to go with you without uttering a word! And, furthermore, you're chucking your career away! Who do you think is going to offer you a job when you come back from Timbuktu? You know as well as I do that the medical hierarchy don't approve of nonconformist breaks like the one you're proposing.'

'Then stuff the medical hierarchy!' he said vehemently. 'And I disagree. Lots of people have worked abroad and come back to find jobs—and the kind of people who wouldn't employ me because I hadn't stuck to some rigid career pattern they'd laid out for me are not the kind of people I'd want to be working with anyway!'

'Leo, please reconsider,' she pleaded. 'Think of the opportunity you've been given. Think what it could mean to us. We wouldn't have to move, and I can keep my job on. We've been happy together here, you know we have. Why spoil it?'

'Darling, we're young, healthy and free. What's to spoil?'

'I want to stay here,' she said stubbornly. 'I don't think that we should just turn our noses up at a good opportunity.' She caught his hand. 'Just think of it, Leo—Dr Marlow's house is on the market—we could afford to buy it. It's a beautiful house—I've always loved it, and you will, too.'

'Go on, Jenny,' he answered in a strange voice. 'What else would you like me to do?'

She couldn't understand the tone of his voice. 'Meaning just what?'

'Meaning that I'm not just some convenient appendage who's slotted in nicely into your old life! I am *not* Harry Marlow—I am Leo Trentham! I want us to build a new life—together. Don't you understand?'

Her voice was cool. 'I don't think that being dragged off to the middle of nowhere is quite how *I* would define building a new life together.'

'I'm not dragging you anywhere!' he exploded. 'I was hoping that you'd want to come with me.'

'You haven't even discussed it with me.'

'Good God, woman—what do you think we're doing at the moment?'

And suddenly her temper flared, too. 'This isn't a discussion, Leo—it's a superfluous talk! You've already made your mind up, haven't you?'

There was a long pause. His voice, when he eventually spoke, was very quiet. 'Yes. Yes. I have.' The deep brown eyes were troubled. 'It's something that I have to do, Jenny. I had hoped you'd understand. Not to go now would be something that I just couldn't live with.' The strong tanned hand reached out to touch her face, but she pulled away.

'And this is the man who once talked of compromise,' she said bitterly.

'If it's compromise you want then that's what we'll go for,' he said. 'If you're so against coming with me—then will you wait? Two years would——'

'I don't think I want to be involved with a man who can treat life so irresponsibly.'

'Jenny,' he said patiently, 'don't you think you're over-reacting a little?'

'Don't you dare patronise me!' she retorted. The

words came spilling out, giving voice to feelings she'd never dared express in all her childhood years. 'I know what it's like to have lived with someone who wouldn't shoulder his responsibilities—remember? My father——'

For the first time in the whole conversation his voice sounded perfectly controlled. Too controlled. 'I am not your father,' he said flatly.

'No, you're not, but you sound just like him.'

'Oh, for God's sake, Jenny,' he exploded. 'When are you going to stop bringing your parents into everything? This is *your* life, *your* reaction—except that sometimes I don't think you dare react as yourself, only as you've been conditioned to! Your mother did a very successful job on you, didn't she—making sure you would trust no one?'

'Get out,' she said in a low, shaking voice.

He stood up and grabbed his jacket, and she knew a terrifying moment of panic as she realised that he had taken her at her word, and was about to leave.

'Maybe we ought to talk about it in the morning,' he said, 'when our tempers have cooled.'

'There's nothing *to* talk about,' she said tightly, some ancient pride making her form the final words, as if her mouth spoke of its own volition. 'I shan't change my mind.'

He stared at her for a long moment, and she met his gaze unwaveringly. For a second she thought he was about to plead with her, or to try to explain further—there was a brief flare of light in the eyes which she knew so well. Then, like a bulb which had been snapped off, the light died.

'I'll collect my things tomorrow, then,' he said. 'Goodbye.'

And, bending his head to accommodate the low beam of the door, he left.

CHAPTER TWELVE

IN THE morning Jenny thought that she might have dreamt it. She awoke, feeling that something was not quite right, but unsure what. Then she registered that the other side of the bed had not been slept in at the same moment that she recalled the harsh and angry words which had been spoken.

Yet she did not feel desolate, not then. She continued to feel aggrieved—and justified. There could be no future for two people who thought so differently. She had been right all along. All the things her instincts had warned her of about Leo right at the beginning had been proved correct. If only she had followed those instincts. . .

She was on a late duty and the ward was busy. She rushed around, moving beds to prepare for those coming back from Theatre. Than an IVI got blocked and she was busy trying to flush it through, and in the end Leo had to come and re-site it. She asked Daisy Galloway to accompany him, and she didn't care what anyone thought.

She saw him briefly at seven, when he did a ward-round. He was almost glacially polite to her, and that, somehow, shocked her. She had said things to him which she had meant, and indeed still meant, and yet she had not worked through how the reality would seem. She could never have

imagined that Leo could be so cold with her. Even
when they had fallen out on previous occasions,
before the relationship had started, there had been
none of this chilly distance between them. She
realised that she was seeing the death of love. . .

She reached home at ten, and had half imagined
that she would see his motor bike outside, with
the lights on, a fire lit and a smiling Leo waiting
for her, but of course there was no such thing.
And when she had unlocked the door and stepped
inside she blinked, for there was something very
different, and she couldn't for the life of her work
out what it was.

And then she realised. He had gone. All his
things had gone. She ran upstairs to her wardrobe,
to where he had kept sweaters and shirts and
trousers, and every single garment had been
removed. Every single trace of him had vanished,
as though he had never lived there. She didn't
realise how much of him had been present in her
surroundings until he was no longer there. Not a
solitary coffee-cup or a plate gave evidence of his
presence.

He had left his key, not on the table, but on the
small locker beside her bed, next to a book she had
been reading, and that, more than anything else,
upset her.

She stared at the key for a long while, and then
she began to cry.

She tried to talk sense into herself. Of course she
missed him, that was only natural, and, besides,

he wasn't showing any signs of missing *her*, was he? Hadn't India Westwood taken great pains and pleasure to point out that Leo had been spotted leaving Theatres with Alison Banbury?

She had meant what she'd said. She didn't want to throw away everything she had worked for. One day she could be glad that she had made this decision—she would be better off without him.

She knew that he had handed his notice in. Everyone knew. The reasons why circulated like wildfire round the small hospital and, once they found out that he was planning to work in the Third World, his already shining reputation grew by leaps and bounds. Anyone would have thought that he was a knight going off in search of the Holy Grail, thought Jenny crossly as she heaped butter on to a baked potato in the canteen.

She had been about to bite in hungrily when she saw him enter the room, accompanied by Alison Banbury and Andy McClaren. Suddenly she felt sick. She saw India Westwood looking triumphantly in her direction. She put her knife and fork down.

Leo was just about to join the queue when he noticed her sitting there, and for a long moment their eyes held. She half thought that he was about to approach her, but then she heard Alison Banbury's strident tones.

'Get me the ham omelette, will you, Leo? I'll go and bag us a table.'

Jenny knew that she had to get out of there. She walked out of the canteen with her head held high and went outside to the bench among the flower-beds which surrounded the old tennis courts.

She pulled her navy cloak around her shoulders. The sunshine was bright, but she felt cold. She had just under three weeks until he left. She had made the right decision—they could never have been happy. Before he had arrived, causing chaos in her life, she hadn't felt the need to have a man around. She had been contented.

Contented. She gave a low snort of derision. She could never imagine feeling anything as safe and comforting as contented ever again. Certainly never while Leo Trentham remained in the hospital to haunt her with the memories of their intimacy. And once you had removed that from their relationship—what remained? Basic incompatibility, that was what.

The more she reasoned with herself, the surer she became. If ever she did settle down with someone it would have to be someone who shared her goals, her aims, her ambitions, and her view of the world.

Leo brought in an enormous chocolate cake on his second to last day, together with a magnum of champagne to be shared out with the nurses and all the patients whose drugs allowed them to partake of alcohol!

Jenny couldn't bear to join in and excused herself quietly to Jackie Graham.

'It's almost half-past four,' she said, once she had handed over. 'And I'm off.'

Jackie looked bemused. 'What's happened

between you two?' she asked. 'We all thought everything was going swimmingly.'

'I don't really want to talk about it. It's all over now, and that's for the best,' replied Jenny, managing to produce a tight little smile which didn't fool Jackie Graham for a minute.

It was the longest evening of Jenny's entire life, and at nine the phone rang.

It was Leo. 'I want to talk to you,' he said without preamble.

She thought of everything she had been telling herself for the last few weeks. She thought of Alison Banbury. She steeled herself. 'I think we've said everything there is to be said.'

Perhaps if he'd pleaded. But there again, he wasn't a man who would plead.

'I don't agree,' came the deep voice. 'But there's no point in arguing the toss if your mind's made up.' A pause. 'Goodbye, Jenny.'

'Goodbye, Leo,' and then she put the phone down quickly before the tears came.

She had arranged the off-duty so that she had a day off on what was to be his final day. She drove for miles to the city, parking her car and planning to shop to her heart's content, but she couldn't summon up the slightest bit of interest in the goods and wares which littered the shops.

At one point she saw an Oxfam poster with the face of an emaciated child staring down at her, reproach in the dark eyes which for a second resembled the eyes of the man she loved. *Had* loved, she corrected herself automatically. She found herself thinking of all the merchandise she had seen that day, started imagining Christmas, and the rampant consumerism which would envelop them all, as it did every year. Vapid and transient pleasures they would seem to Leo, she thought, out working in the most primitive of conditions. One half of the world starving, while the other half revelled in over-indulgence. . . She shook her head a little and began to walk back to the car, her hands empty.

It was dark when she got back, and she saw at once that Leo had left his cottage—it had that uncurtained, empty look about it once more. But, even if she hadn't seen that, as soon as she stepped from her car Jack, the landlord of the pub where he'd taken her on their first date, informed her that, 'The doctor's gone—'e came in and said goodbye earlier. There'll be a few around these parts who'll miss him, I'd say.'

The blue eyes glanced at her shrewdly, but Jenny managed a smile. 'I'm sure they will, Jack,' she agreed. 'He was a very good doctor.'

But once Leo had actually gone she began to realise just how much *she* missed him. It was as if his continued presence at the hospital had allowed her to forget that he was no longer part of her life. Once he had gone the loneliness she felt became unbearable.

She started to play records that he had liked, to sit and mooch around the cottage. For the first time in her life she had difficulty sleeping—not just on the occasional night, but every night.

On more than one occasion she put her hand out towards the telephone, thinking that she could try to contact him, but something stopped her—whether it was a certainty that they were better off apart, or the fear of being rejected, she didn't know, but the call was never made.

Two weeks to the day of his departure there was a sharp rap on the door at seven-thirty.

Her heart started fluttering like a tiny bird trapped in a cage, as she leapt to her feet.

She pulled open the door and started in surprise. The smiling tanned face was at once curiously well known, and yet unfamiliar.

'Well?' dimpled the woman. 'Is that any way to treat your old staff nurse? Aren't you going to invite me in?'

Jenny beamed. 'Hello, Judy,' she said, hugging the middle-aged woman. 'You can't believe how pleased I am to see you!'

CHAPTER THIRTEEN

JUDY COLLINS stood in the small sitting-room of the cottage regarding Jenny critically.

'You look awful,' she observed.

'Thanks,' said Jenny wryly.

'Too thin, and too pale. Is this what love does for you?'

'Love? What do you. . .?'

Judy smiled as she put her handbag down on the table. 'You and Dr Trentham. I hear you're love's young dream!'

'I. . .' Jenny opened her mouth to deny it, and then, to her horror, she began to cry, breaking down completely and ending up sobbing in the arms of the older woman.

Judy said nothing, merely making soothing noises until the sobs had subsided into sniffs, and Jenny began blowing her nose noisily into a handkerchief.

'I'm sorry,' she sniffed, 'I don't know what's the matter with me—I never used to cry.' She said it in some astonishment, as if surprised that she was capable of displaying such florid emotions.

'I've always thought that you bottled things up far too much,' said Judy candidly. 'You used to do it as a child—it isn't healthy, in my opinion. Now dry your eyes and sit down and tell me what's been happening. And don't look so desolate—I'm sure if you've had a lover's tiff it's nothing that can't be sorted out.'

Jenny shook her head slowly. 'No,' she said. 'It's too late for that. Too much has been said.'

'Let me be the judge of that,' suggested Judy. 'Tell me what has happened.'

Jenny scrubbed at her eyes with the handkerchief. It was difficult to know where to start. 'When I first met Leo——' her voice faltered a little '—I hated him. I thought that he was everything I despised in a man—impulsive, unconventional, emotional. And yet. . .' she bit her lip '. . .and yet I was attracted to him at the same time.'

'Sounds fairly normal to me!' smiled Judy.

Jenny tried to give a wan smile, and failed. 'Well, we started going out and things happened very quickly. We fell in love, he moved in here, and asked me to marry him—and I agreed.'

'Sounds perfect!'

'Oh, it was, Judy—absolutely. And then he went and ruined everything.' She told Judy about the roadside amputation and about the boy who had died of the fat embolism, of how profoundly it had affected Leo.

'It ended with his being offered the senior reg job at Denbury and St Martin's, when he calmly told me that he wasn't going to accept it, that he was going off to work in the Third World for two years, and that he wanted me to go with him!'

Judy looked unimpressed. 'So?'

Jenny looked at her in exasperation. 'Well, don't you realise? I'd been right to think we were unsuited! I'm happy here, and I'd like to stay—I don't want a mixed-up unpredictable future. I'm not like that, Judy—you know that. I like order, and calm. Security.'

Judy ignored this. 'Do you love him?'

'Yes. . . No.' She lifted her hands in the air. 'Yes, of course I love him. But love on its own isn't enough, is it?'

'Says who?'

Jenny sighed. 'Well, my mother said, for one. Look at what happened to her and Daddy. They were totally unsuited, and in the end he left her.'

'She drove him away,' said Judy quietly.

Jenny looked up. 'What did you say?'

'She did exactly what you're trying to do to Leo now. She trapped him in a life he didn't want; she tried to mould him, to make him conform to what she wanted him to be. Only Leo has the sense not to let you do it to him. Your father didn't, and in the end he took the only route he could, and left.'

'She should have married someone more like herself—someone like Harry Marlow.'

'And why do you think she didn't?'

'Perhaps he never asked her.'

Judy smiled. 'Harry Marlow was sweet on your mother for years. That's not the reason.'

'They couldn't have got married—because Mummy never divorced.'

'Yes!' said Judy triumphantly. 'And why? Because she still loved your father. Because she never gave up hope that he would come back to her one day. But he never did.'

Jenny looked dazed. 'How do you know all this?'

'She was my friend,' said Judy simply. 'She told me all kinds of things which she could never have told you, her daughter. Listen,' she took Jenny's hand, 'what a boring place the world would be if we only married people who we thought were "suitable"! If you love Leo—then go to him. What's your alternative? Look at the miserable state you're in. Can you contemplate a life without him? Can you?'

'But it's too late,' said Jenny desperately. 'He's gone.'

'Then find him,' said Judy firmly. 'Find him and go to him. Tonight if you can. Don't waste any more time. Time is too precious.'

Time *was* precious, and that, she suddenly realised, was the whole reason for Leo's wanting to use his surgical skills to help others. He wanted to use his youth and his energy to help others. Really help. And she had told him, mealy-mouthed, to accept the dull safe option. Sentencing him to a lifetime of stultifying conformity. Would he ever forgive her for that? She didn't know, but it was a chance she had to take.

'I know where his parents live,' she said suddenly. 'They must know where he is. And tomorrow's my day off.'

'Then go for it—and send me a postcard!'

Once Judy had left Jenny got on the phone to

directory enquiries, praying inwardly that the Trenthams weren't ex-directory.

Leo's mother answered the phone. Jenny thought that she sounded slightly cool.

'He leaves next week,' she said. 'He's staying at his brother's flat until then.'

'Please. . .' said Jenny breathlessly, 'can I have the address?'

There was a pause. Mrs Trentham was not particularly pleased to see her son looking so wretched over some girl. She had thought that the affair was over. Obviously it was not. She gave a sigh, knowing that she shouldn't interfere. They had tried to interfere in Leo's life too many times in the past, and all it had ever caused was bitterness.

'It's in Knightsbridge,' she said. 'Have you got a pen?'

Jenny changed into jeans and a warm sweater, and, turning off all the lights and locking the door, made her way out to the car. Judy was right. She should go to him tonight. She mustn't waste any more time. If he would have her. . .

It was a dark, blustery night, and she was reminded of the night when they had travelled to perform the amputation. Even on the subject of the motor bike she had been totally intransigent. He had driven safely in the most appalling conditions, yet she had still refused to ever ride pillion again—and he had tolerated that with smiling affection.

He was kind and good and true, and she had

been too blind to recognise that these were the things that mattered, that houses and jobs came second. She put her main-beam headlights on, trying to get better vision ahead through the driving rain.

It was a long, long drive. She hadn't left until gone nine, and by the time she drove into the outskirts of London it was rapidly approaching midnight. She got hopelessly lost, and in the end managed to buy a street directory from a store which was open all night. Eventually she passed the glorious bright windows of Harrods, and, three streets away, found the block of flats she was searching for.

It was terribly impressive. A heavy revolving door and thick dark red carpet with glossy wood panelling everywhere. The ancient lift with its heavy iron railings looked far too cumbersome to manoeuvre, and so she took the stairs, running all the way up to the third floor until a thought struck her and her steps slowed.

It was now almost one o'clock. What if he was not alone? What if he was in bed with someone else? She had no claim on him now. The thought made fine beads of sweat break out on her forehead. She had to see him. She couldn't turn back now. Even if it was for the last time, she had to see him.

She rang the doorbell. There was no answer and no light shining from under the door. What if he was out? She had nowhere to go. She would just have to sit on the doorstep and wait for him. She stood and waited for another minute, then rang once more.

She heard a sound, and her heart raced. A light was on, and she could hear footsteps approaching. What if it was his brother? How would she be able to explain why she was standing, damp and bedraggled, on his doorstep in the middle of the night?

The door opened. It was Leo. He stood staring at her. It was strange to see him surrounded by such luxury, but he looked the same. He was bare-chested and wore a pair of jeans. She saw the faint shadow on his chin, saw the narrowed brown eyes scrutinising her, and she felt almost dizzy with love and desire, but his face gave nothing away.

She didn't think he was going to make this easy for her, and she didn't think she deserved him to, either. She must just tell him the truth.

'Leo, I'm sorry. I was so wrong. I love you and I've missed you. Terribly. And I want to come with you. If it's not too late.'

He relaxed then, and gave her that wide careless smile, and her heart skipped a beat. He grabbed her hand and pulled her inside, straight into his arms, and kicked the door shut.

'Come here,' he told her. 'This kind of neigh-bourhood isn't used to passionate declarations of love at this time of the morning! Did you drive here tonight, you crazy woman?'

'Yes,' she sobbed into his bare chest. 'I've missed you so much—can you ever forgive me?'

'Only if you stop crying so that I can kiss you.'

She actually thought she'd pass out. It seemed an eternity since she'd felt his lips on hers, and the sensation was almost unbearably exquisite.

'You're soaking,' he murmured. 'I think we'll have to get you out of those wet clothes and into a nice hot bath.'

But they never made it past the floor of the hall. 'Your. . .brother?' she managed to gasp as he tugged at the waistband of her jeans impatiently.

'In Paris,' he muttered as he began to kiss the nape of her neck.

Later she got her bath, and he sat in it with her, the hot soapy bubbles up to their shoulders.

He kissed her slowly. 'So tell me what's happened to make you change your mind?'

'I thought you'd demand an explanation straight away!'

He grinned. 'I had other things on my mind!' His face grew serious. 'I've missed you like hell. All I wanted to do when I saw you again was to make love to you. Do you want to know why? It's a shockingly primitive reason.'

'Tell me,' she whispered.

'I just wanted to re-establish my claim on you—and to wipe away all the bad words.'

'There were a lot of very silly, thoughtless words on my part,' she said. 'I was wrong to try and force you into a life you didn't want, just because of my need for security——'

'Jenny,' he interrupted her, 'I may be impulsive, but I'll always take good care of you; never doubt that for a moment. I love you and I want to cherish you—that's part of the vow we'll be taking when we marry.'

'Oh, Leo!' she cried. 'To think I might have lost you.'

'What made you come?' he asked.

She told him about her conversation with Judy. 'I now realise that there are two sides to every-thing—that my father wasn't necessarily the vil-lain of the piece. There were reasons why he left, and my mother contributed to them.' She glanced at him ruefully. 'Judy says that my mother trapped him, tried to mould him into what she wanted—as I tried to do with you; the difference was that you wouldn't let me!'

He smiled. 'I'm almost as stubborn as you are!'

'More stubborn!'

He lifted her chin very gently. 'But seriously, darling, parents aren't necessarily all good, or all bad—they're bits of both, just like us! They try to influence us because they don't want us to make their mistakes, except that it never works out quite like that—youth is notoriously bad at benefitting from experience! We'll probably be the same with our own children.'

The thought of having his child one day made her feel particularly soppy.

He smiled at the look on her face. 'About that compromise.' He smiled at her tenderly. 'I've been thinking, too. Perhaps I've been too emphatic about things. I still want to go to Zambia, and it's a minimum of two years. Do you remember what I said once before, that, if you were totally against going, you could wait? You could come out and see me as often as you liked. Would you wait for me, Jenny?'

'No, I certainly wouldn't!' she declared firmly. 'I'm coming with you—I'm not letting hundreds of other nurses like Alison Banbury try to get their hands on you!'

He threw back his head and chuckled. 'Oh, Alison Banbury! You're obsessed with Alison Banbury!'

'No,' she retorted, her green eyes flashing fire, 'she was obsessed—with you!'

'I love it when you're jealous,' he teased. 'Come here. Shall we get a special licence and get married next week?'

'Yes, please,' she sighed happily.

'I assume that you'll have to go back and work a month's notice. We'll go down to the VSO offices tomorrow, to arrange for you to join me. Can you deliver babies, by the way?'

'Of course I can!'

'Good. It's a skill I think you're going to be using a lot of out there.'

She let him dry her and wrap her in an enormous fluffy towel, and he put her in his bed and went off to make them some coffee. They lay awake for hours, until daylight began to creep through the curtains. Leo leaned on one elbow and looked down at her.

'I know you think we're unsuited, but I think you're wrong.'

'I think I've been wrong, too,' she whispered. 'You suit me just fine.'

'I love you, Jenny.'

'And I love you.'

'And you're *really* sure about coming to Zambia with me?'

She stroked the dark tangled hair. 'I've discovered a lot of things about myself these past few weeks, but the most important is that I don't care where I live, or what I do, as long as I'm with you.'

And she'd never been so certain of anything in her life.

COMING IN SEPTEMBER

The eagerly awaited new novel from this internationally bestselling author. Lying critically injured in hospital, Liz Danvers implores her estranged daughter to return home and read her diaries. As Sage reads she learns of painful secrets in her mothers hidden past, and begins to feel compassion and a reluctant admiration for this woman who had stood so strongly between herself and the man she once loved. The diaries held the clues to a number of emotional puzzles, but the biggest mystery of all was why Liz had chosen to reveal her most secret life to the one person who had every reason to resent and despise her.

Available: September 1991. Price £4.99

W●RLDWIDE

From: Boots, Martins, John Menzies, W.H. Smith,
Woolworths and other paperback stockists.
Also available from Reader Service, Thornton Road,
Croydon Surrey, CR9 3RU

A special gift for Christmas

Four romantic stories by four of your favourite
authors for you to unwrap and enjoy this
Christmas.

Robyn Donald	STORM OVER PARADISE
Catherine George	BRAZILIAN ENCHANTMENT
Emma Goldrick	SMUGGLER'S LOVE
Penny Jordan	SECOND-BEST HUSBAND

Published on 11th October, 1991   Price: £6.40

MEDICAL  ROMANCE

The books for your enjoyment this month are:

CROCK OF GOLD Angela Devine
SEIZE THE DAY Sharon Wirdnam
LEARNING TO CARE Clare Mackay
FROM SHADOW TO SUNLIGHT Jenny Ashe

♥   ♥   ♥   ♥   ♥

Treats in store!

Watch next month for the following absorbing stories:

A SPECIAL CHALLENGE Judith Ansell
HEART IN CRISIS Lynne Collins
DOCTOR TO THE RESCUE Patricia Robertson
BASE PRINCIPLES Sheila Danton